THE KEY ON EDGE

MICHAEL J. PIATT

Artwork By
Juan Giraldo

Dedicated to the next generation. May they preserve all that is good. May they dare to dream of better and have the fortitude to pursue those dreams.

TABLE OF CONTENTS

PROLOGUE

As the rock was slowly lifted from atop Majestic Mountain, something shiny glinted from underneath. Could it have been a knife? It was balanced perfectly on its edge, defying the forces of gravity.

"This is impossible," breathed Kim, as the light flickered on and off between pitch black and blinding brightness. The glaring edge of that metallic object pierced straight through her eyes. As she bent down to pick it up, she realized it was not a knife blade at all. It was a key, meticulously decorated with intricate scrollwork that one would expect might open an entire kingdom of riches. As she grasped it in her hand, she felt a certain pull of its own against her, as if it were somehow connected to the peaceful inner earth surrounded by the crusty world around it. The top of Majestic Mountain was no ordinary place, encapsulated by the mundane.

These unexplainable events were orchestrated by the Sharefield Gang performing in the Central High School play of *The Script*. It was a production that would influence the very fabric of their lives. A story that would manifest itself in numerous ways throughout their ninth-grade year. Turns out, this was no ordinary year by any measure.

I

THE SCHOOL PLAY

It was a warm spring day in Sharefield. The gang was anxious and mentally preparing itself for the debut of their school production that very evening. It was a nerve-wracking thought that all their parents, teachers, relatives, and friends would be in attendance, scrutinizing them.

The students had been practicing relentlessly over the previous several months for this day, but when it was high time to show what they were capable of, the jitters were wreaking havoc.

Sharefield is a small community with just one high school for grades nine through twelve. The six first-year students created this 'gang' during early childhood and, since then, have been practically inseparable.

It was Kim's idea to get involved in the theater production. She was adventurous and liked to take charge—a natural leader. She was well-organized and had a knack for making everyone feel important.

Admittedly, getting the whole gang to sign up took a little convincing, especially Lucia, who tended to be the shyest of the bunch, but she was smart and always thought things through before taking action—a good person to have around in times of crisis.

Kim discovered that the playwright was an unknown local man who wrote this masterpiece based on a journey just outside of Sharefield, up Majestic Mountain.

What convinced the gang was the fact that this play was about the mountain the gang was most familiar with.

She promoted the idea of the production to the gang so that everyone felt like it would be a source of pride for their community.

Failure to take part in a script of such local significance would be disrespectful to the school and all it stood for. After Kim was done with her solemn speech, every gang member felt the same way and was driven to show their school spirit.

Nate tried out for the lead. Instead, he was assigned a strong supporting role as the assistant to the guide for the expedition up the mountain. That was fine by him. Nate had his opinions all right but tended to go with the flow and avoid confrontation. He was observant and somewhat of a philosopher, not one to push for change.

Kim was cast in the rightful lead role as the guide, and Victor played Kim's younger brother, who was to accompany his older sister on the journey. Victor, the voice of reason in real life, was a stabilizing force.

Anthony had the part of managing the local store where all the gear was purchased for the expedition, while Lucia was thrilled to be assigned to oversee all the costumes for the performance.

Of course, as the plot was written, it turned into a bit of an exaggeration to refer to it as an expedition. It was a three-day adventure hike up the mountain, where discoveries were made about various wildlife and plant species. That is not exactly the way things turned out.

Sure, there was drama among the hikers, as one might expect over a three-day journey. Someone always didn't like the food or wanted to take a different route. The group got lost three times on the journey, and had it not been for the magic compass, they would never have found their way!

That's where Dion came in. He was the techie of the group, so his job was to oversee the special effects of the play. He had to make the compass light up in the right direction whenever the expedition was at odds as to which way to go.

The mission was to find a magical key, supposedly left by an old man many years ago, at the very top of the mountain.

Many others had tried to search for the key before but could never locate it.

In the play, the key is found.

The production ends without telling exactly what the key is for. It leaves the audience wondering what the sequel might tell of this mysterious find.

The case evoked excitement in the audience as they journeyed up the mountain. The audience was fully engaged in mystery, suspense, and a good dose of humor—especially from Anthony. In addition to running the local store for outfitter gear, he was also the expedition coordinator. His job was to ensure the hikers had tents, sleeping bags, food, and other necessary supplies at every step along the journey.

In real life, as in the production, he was so funny that even when things got mixed up, no one got upset because they were too busy laughing. He had a natural talent for putting everyone at ease with his offbeat sense of humor.

Well, it was three o'clock, and classes were finished for the day. The big debut was all set for that very evening. There were only a few hours left for preparation. Ms. Jill Brock, the teacher in charge of the school production, checked to ensure everything was in order.

Under her guidance, the students had been practicing for months. The entire school was now buzzing with activity as the stage was prepared for the first act. Lucia had laid out all the costumes. The time was finally near.

Everyone was to go home for dinner with their families before returning later that evening.

"I'm so ready for this performance," Nate said to his friends as he walked out of school. "We're going to nail it." At the same time, he had a nervous feeling in his stomach because the whole town would be watching. He did not eat much that evening.

The gang was back at school at six o'clock sharp. As the crowd of friends and loved ones began to fill the gymnasium—turned into a theater—the cast put on their costumes, set the stage for the opening act, and readied themselves for their big debut.

Ms. Brock could sense everyone felt a little tense, but the students jumped into action as soon as the curtain opened. They commanded the stage like well-oiled machines preprogrammed to do exactly what they had done a thousand times before.

It didn't even look like a debut!

They had practiced their lines and knew the dance routines so well they could almost do them in their sleep. The same went for the prop switches and costume changes.

The actors went through the first act as if they were all singing one long song in unison. Their performance was flawless.

The audience showed their appreciation with applause and cheering support for all the students, who surprised even themselves with a near-perfect first act.

During intermission, the cast members refreshed themselves with cold drinks and fruit bar snacks. They caught their breath as they readied themselves for the second half. They shared the goal of showing the town of Sharefield what this ninth-grade class was capable of.

At this time, the Sharefield Gang was most grateful to Kim for suggesting they get involved in theater. Although they had second thoughts during the long hours of practice leading up to this moment, everyone felt it was worth it now.

The second act started off as flawlessly as the first. Everything was progressing like clockwork. In this act, the hikers got lost several times going up Majestic Mountain, but the compass always lit up on cue, thanks to Dion showing the way, as the journey continued. On top of Majestic Mountain, the atmosphere turned misty, again thanks to a water vapor sprayer Dion was controlling.

The mountain explorers tried to locate the magic key strategically placed under a large rock but to no avail.

Per *The Script*, Kim came upon the rock. Then, everyone stood around her as she grabbed one side and tilted it up.

There, she saw something strange that was *not* in *The Script*.

Kim found the key under the rock, balanced perfectly on its edge.

How was this possible? she thought.

This was not what happened in practice. She picked it up and held it in her hand. She had a bizarre feeling it was pushing against her hand with a force much greater than its weight.

Suddenly, all the lights on the stage went off and, a moment later, flickered back on. This happened three times. Some in the audience thought it was part of the play, a special effects thing, but the kids on the stage knew that wasn't the case. They were left stunned.

Nate thought, *What magical force could have caused this unexplainable plunge into total darkness? Is the world still upright?*

Ms. Brock motioned to continue despite the confusion the intermittent lightning induced in the cast and spectators alike. So, they did their very best to recover without incident.

During the rest of the play, there were a few missed queues and mistaken lines since everyone was a bit shaken up. The timing of the light incident was too perfect to be coincidental. The students got through to the end of the play, where the special key was brought down from the mountain and stored in a local safe bank deposit box, number 395. To keep it safe for whatever was to come of it.

The audience was thrilled with the performance, although some were still weirded out. Total darkness during a theater presentation can be uncomfortable, to say the least. They gave all the students a standing ovation that seemed to the cast to last forever. Everyone involved in the production smiled and felt satisfied, knowing they had completed something challenging.

Backstage, Ms. Brock commended them for their team effort. "None of you could have pulled this off on your own, but together, the talents and abilities of each unique individual contributed to its overall success."

Dion remarked, "I learned that having the courage to move forward into something unknown can have tremendous personal rewards."

It occurred to Lucia that the emotional excitement of this new experience somehow increased her awareness of everything around her. "This production has created a memory that will stay with me for some time to come."

Kim was particularly satisfied with the outcome of the production. As Dion put it, "It was Kim who encouraged the rest of us to participate."

Kim merely blushed and smiled.

2

THE FIELD TRIP

Now that the play's excitement was over, the gang looked forward to the end of the school year and their rewarding summer break.

As compensation for all their work during the year, their teachers planned a field trip to the base of Majestic Mountain, where their school play was based.

One crisp spring morning in late May, the students packed lunches in their backpacks, got on the school bus, and headed for the now-famous-among-the-students mountain. They could see its smoky, mystical-looking peak even from the bus, miles from the base. The entire class was looking out the windows and snapping pictures with their phones while Anthony sang 'On Top of Old Smokey.'

The bus was so noisy with chatter that Arthur, the driver, had to ask everyone to quiet down so he could hear if a train was approaching on the railroad tracks they were about to cross.

Once they reached the mountain base, everyone quickly exited the bus. The crisp air filled the students with the energy to engage and explore.

"The funny thing is that the mountain does not look quite so big now that we are right beside it," said Victor.

One of the teachers and their guide for the day, Ms. Jenkins, explained that it is a matter of perspective.

"You are not seeing the entire mountain from this vantage point," she explained.

By this time, it was mid-morning. The entire class followed along the trail that led them into the woods. Ms. Jenkins knew the area very well. Many classes before had made a similar pilgrimage to the mountain as a school-sponsored field trip.

Around lunchtime, the roar of water in the distance filled the air. It was beating against their eardrums like being in the first row of a heavy metal band concert. One student described it as thunder over the top of a charging herd of buffalo. All of that made sense since they could hardly hear themselves talk.

As they rounded the bend, they saw a beautiful waterfall cascading down the mountain cliff into the lagoon below, fed by The Wandering River. It was quite a sight to behold.

As Nate looked at the cascading falls, he gasped, "Nature is amazing!"

Standing beside him, Dion said, "A minute ago, we were in the shadows of the woods. Now, we suddenly have this glorious sight in front of us."

Ms. Jenkins told the class that this gorge was formed before the time of the dinosaurs and was still in motion due to natural erosion from the mighty waterfall.

Victor said, "It's hard to imagine something as massive and stable as a cliff would move. But I guess over an extended period of time, things change, even though you don't notice it happening from day to day."

Anthony, who was equally impressed, referred to it as the 'Wonder Wear River.' He was always coming up with corny names for things. It was part of his personality.

The class stopped at the base of the falls for lunch. Mist from the waterfall landing in the lagoon below rose high and blew over the students, keeping them cool while they ate. Kim remarked, "This is just like the mist machine in the play that Dion controlled at the top of Majestic Mountain."

Anthony referred to the mist as 'Crash Splash.'

After lunch, Ms. Jenkins stood up and said, "It's time to take a class picture."

Dion looked at the beautiful scenery surrounding them and had an idea. He wanted the picture to be unique so he could look back and remember his ninth-grade classmates.

He noticed a flat recess and what appeared to be a cave directly behind the falls.

That would make a great picture, he thought.

"Maybe we can all stand on that large, flat plateau leading into the cave behind the falls for our picture," he suggested.

Everyone thought that was a great idea, so each student climbed, single file, over the rocks leading to the plateau behind the falls. The class also wanted Ms. Jenkins in the picture, so they asked Arthur to take their picture. He happily obliged.

As everyone maneuvered to be seen clearly in the photo, Dion noticed something behind him. The sun shining through the falls just after midday revealed a reflective object inside the entrance to the cave. The water interrupted the sun's rays, so the shiny object seemed to pulse the reflected light in groups of three.

"That's strange," Dion furrowed his brows, but no one paid much attention to him. Everyone was still moving about, preparing for the great photo shoot.

Three flashes went off. The kids readjusted themselves before three flashes went off again. Standing in the back row, Dion ducked down and snuck away from the photo shoot after the first couple of shots. Much to his surprise, as he moved toward the flashing object, he saw it was a key of some sort. He closed his eyes and looked again but could hardly believe what was before him.

It was leaning against a rock, on its edge, so that it would reflect the sunlight. He quickly picked it up and slid it into his pocket, then returned to the group, missing only one of the shots Arthur had set up for the class.

Dion was excited to have this strange object in his possession, but he honestly didn't know what to do with it. He referred to it as his 'keep.'

Throughout the rest of the field trip, he dared not take it out of his pocket for fear of being discovered before he had a chance to examine it closely. *Was it something magical or just an old key that someone lost long ago? Should I tell the teacher or keep it to myself?*

The rest of the school day, he was a bit preoccupied with the possibilities of what he had found behind the million-year-old waterfall. He just kept thinking, *could it possibly relate to the school play somehow?*

That evening, Dion pulled the key from his pocket and scrutinized it in the privacy of his own room. He was amazed. As far as he could tell, it looked exactly like the key in the school production.

How could this even be possible? he thought to himself. This was too crazy to be a random accident.

* * *

The final days of the school year were uneventful. The class had already finished their final exams the week before. The Sharefield Gang would not see many other students until the start of the next year, but the six of them would usually stick together like glue over the summer months.

Summers in the small town of Sharefield were full of barbecues, pool parties, and organized sports. Kim pitched on a softball team, while Lucia enjoyed volleyball. Dion was tall for his age and lived to play basketball. Nate was more of a soccer player, but only during the school season this year.

The way he looked at it, summer was a time for adventure.

Adventure it would turn out to be, indeed.

3

SUMMER BREAK

On the first day of summer vacation, the gang went to Kim's house to talk and reminisce about the year past. Kim's basement was their private meeting place. It was where they could spend time together and be themselves. There was a big table down there for cards and board games.

Their host had set out several jigsaw puzzles, thinking her friends might want to assemble one. Everyone in the gang had an opinion about which puzzle they should work on as a group. Some of the puzzles looked easier than others.

Nate said, "I really like the boats in the harbor puzzle. Someday, I want to learn how to sail."

Victor said, "The water in that puzzle will be quite a challenge because all the pieces are the same color."

Kim said, "I want to make the New York skyline picture with Dion. New York is such an exciting place. I hope I can visit there someday."

After much debate, they finally decided to start all three puzzles and work in groups of two in separate areas of the large table.

Nate worked with Victor on the boats in the harbor puzzle while Lucia and Anthony teamed up together to assemble a medieval castle scene. Victor was right about the boat harbor picture; filling in the pieces in the water proved difficult. All three groups were making good progress.

After each pair finished their respective puzzles' outer frame, things started getting slightly ridiculous. The unused pieces spread farther apart as everyone tried to figure out how to position them into their puzzle.

Before anyone knew it, the pieces of all three puzzles were thoroughly mixed up on the table. Everyone started to laugh at the predicament they found themselves in.

"What the heck," Dion said. "Why don't we see what we can put together using any piece that fits into any one of the puzzles."

"Now that sounds like fun!" agreed Anthony, as Lucia smiled at him.

Being the funny guy he was, Anthony started to put together a sailboat in the moat around the castle. Others were adding medieval bricks near the top of the Empire State Building. Everyone had a great time creating images without regard to their context.

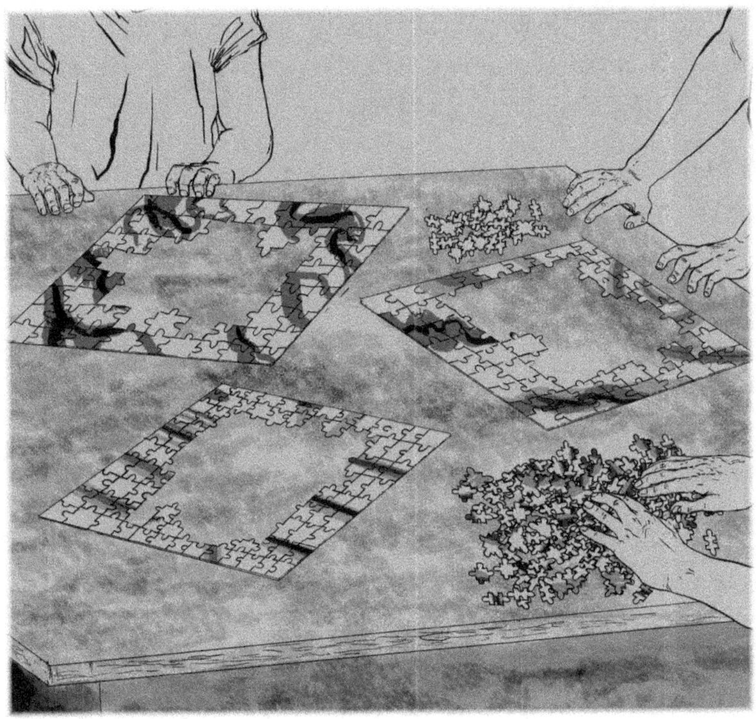

The afternoon passed by in a flash. By dinnertime, they had completed all three puzzles in proper abstract form, with unlikely image combinations in the most bizarre positions.

Nate said, "Despite our rather unorthodox method, these all turned out rather well, I would say."

Kim nodded, saying, "I have to get a picture," as she captured an image of the Statue of Liberty placed on the deck of a yacht in a harbor with a medieval drawbridge that led nowhere.

She said, "Dion, that was brilliant."

The first big event of the summer was set for the weekend after Memorial Day at Ms. Jenkins's parents' house. They had a big farm just outside of town.

Dion had made a rocket for a school project but never had the chance to launch it. He planned to take it to the farm and shoot it off for everyone to see, treating the town to a mini fireworks display!

Everyone showed up for the barbecue around noon. Folks took turns on the grill cooking some of the most delicious entrees imaginable. Each family brought a side dish and various condiments. The food was mouthwateringly delicious.

As Anthony bit into an ear of corn, it shot what he called 'corn juice' in all directions.

Anthony told Lucia, "There is something about being out here on the farm that makes everything taste better."

Kim replied, "Maybe because everything is so fresh, and the air is filled with flavors off the grill."

To which Dion replied, "It makes you feel more alive."

After they finished eating, Dion set up his rocket in the middle of a vast field. He was very proud of it and wanted to share the launch with a big audience. There's no doubt there's a certain thrill in watching a rocket of any size shoot skyward toward the clouds. Dion considered it might reach a high altitude before drifting back to Earth. As he set up the launching pad, he remarked, "We need to ensure plenty of space around the launching area for the rocket's safe return." Dion had rigged up an electric igniter so he wouldn't have to stand too close to the rocket at takeoff. The rocket was about a foot and a half tall. It contained a parachute supposed to deploy at maximum height, allowing it to float back to Earth.

As everyone gathered to watch, there was a lot of chatter among the crowd about how high the rocket might fly. Then Dion announced, "It is time. Everyone yell at once. Three, two, one, blast off!"

He hit the launch button right on time, but nothing happened. He hit it again, but nothing happened still. The spectators were expressing disappointment now. They began to disperse as Dion, feeling quite dejected, examined the electric launch system.

Kim comforted him saying, "Dion, you gave it your best shot."

Dion replied, "Except that it was not a shot at all."

Lucia had just seen a TV show on the tiny particles that made up all matter, so she had an idea! In her mind, she pretended she was a small electron traveling through the wire from the remote igniter to the rocket. When she arrived, she realized the wire was nice and thick, so the electron would easily pass through it.

"That's the problem!" she yelled.

"What is the problem?" asked Victor.

Lucia explained, "The wire is supposed to generate enough heat to cause the rocket's fuse to light. The wire must be too thick."

She took off and ran to Dion to tell him that she thought the wire on the end of the launcher next to the rocket fuse needed to be thinner so the electrical current passing through it would create more friction.

Dion just looked at her kind of funny for that lengthy explanation that did not make sense to him, but her expression was so convincing he decided to try it anyway. There was nothing to lose.

He unraveled the wire next to the fuse and used just one strand of the original wire where it would contact the rocket's fuse. He put the launcher back together and tested the button. Much to his amazement, the wire touching the fuse started to glow red-hot!

"Lucia, you did it!" he exclaimed. "What tremendous insight."

Dion liked to pride himself on his technical abilities, but this time, Lucia came to the rescue and solved the rocket launcher problem.

He gathered everyone at the barbecue together for a second launch attempt. Together, everyone started yelling the countdown again.

"Ten, nine, eight . . ."

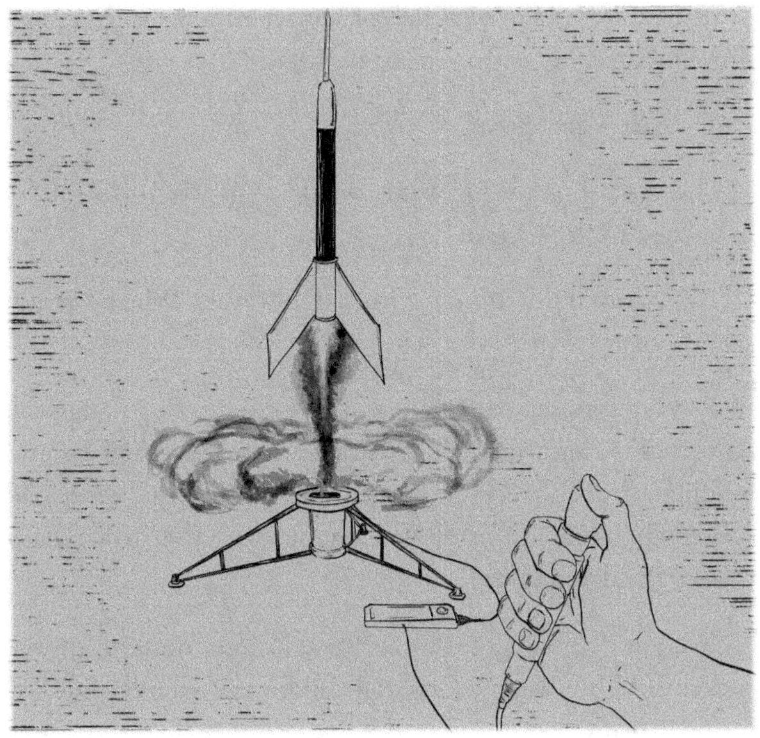

This time, the remote launcher worked flawlessly. The rocket shot toward the heavens like a cannon, with a mild *swoooooosh*, leaving a white trail of smoke stagnant in the atmosphere behind it.

"Wow! Now there is a tall tail of smoking guns," said Anthony.

Within seconds, the rocket was out of sight. Everyone was squinting to look up into the sun. There was no sign of it nor the beautiful red parachute slowly drifting to the ground. It simply disappeared into the afternoon sky.

The gang stood in disbelief for several minutes as the crowd thinned again, returning to the barbecue.

Dion was devastated.

"I am thrilled that it went so high, but what could have happened to it?" he muttered.

All Nate could think of for a reply was, "Maybe it got carried away by the jet stream."

It was supposed to be a joke, but Dion was not laughing. As the crowd returned to the barbecue site, those left behind tending to the food were excited. Evidently, the wind had shifted direction just after launch, sending the rocket back toward the cooking area.

Everyone there got to see the glorious descent of the rocket, held by strings to its brightly colored red parachute, as it slowly drifted to the ground.

What a fantastic sight!

Coincidentally, the returning craft landed directly on the picnic table where Dion and the Sharefield Gang sat.

As Dion returned to the eating area, everyone yelled at him, "Look, there is your rocket." He was speechless. He picked up the rocket and held it high for everyone to see as they clapped in appreciation. He was grinning from ear to ear.

Kim remarked, "See Dion, you have entertained everyone here with your rocket. You did give it your best shot after all."

The successful launch, thanks to Lucia, added to the already festive mood of the party. The music started up as everyone danced and clowned around.

Anthony was doing the 'Blastoff Boogie,' with his arms extending straight up over his head, moving from side to side.

He said that this was his version of 'Rocket Roll.'

His friends shook their heads and laughed.

4

PLANNING FOR MAJESTIC MOUNTAIN

Sitting around that day at the barbecue, Anthony, Victor, Dion, and Nate decided to hike up Majestic Mountain. It was a three-day round trip, so the boys had to camp on the mountain.

Kim and Lucia were already involved in sports for the summer but were supportive of the idea. They even volunteered to help prepare supplies if the boys were allowed to go.

Dion proposed it to his parents, saying, "We would be careful. It would be an excursion we would remember for a long time." However, no matter what he said, Dion's parents were against the idea, thinking it would be too dangerous. That was disappointing, but Nate and Victor accepted the situation. Dion did not. He kept making the point to his parents that they would be safe, and they could stay in touch with them all the time through their cell phones.

After further discussion, Victor's older brother, Brandon, and his friend Phillip, agreed to follow closely behind the boys. Phillip was about to graduate from Central High School that year while Brandon was studying forestry at the State University. They were both accustomed to the outdoors and knew how to survive in the wild. The deal the older boys made with the gang was to make the journey with the boys but to always stay a couple of hours of travel time behind them on the trail.

This way, the first-time hikers could enjoy their freedom and yet be able to rely on assistance from Brandon and Phillip in case of an emergency. The boys' parents agreed to the trip under those conditions.

The gang would be taking enough supplies for the entire journey so they should not have to rely on anything from others, realizing that you just can't be too safe.

Climbing Majestic Mountain would be a daring feat and a fantastic journey from the boy's perspective. They figured they would learn a lot regardless of the outcome. It would allow them to live out their real-life school play for a few days.

The more they thought about it, they realized how much preparation was required for a trip like this. Nate's head was spinning with excitement for the journey and concern over the long list of items they would need to take. He added to his list every day, as did his friends. Dion suggested they each compile a list and then compare so that if one forgot something, another might have remembered it. That worked out very well as they compared their lists every few days before the trip.

The boys also needed to learn about the mountain terrain to navigate their way. Brandon suggested they plan a primary and alternate route in case of unexpected problems.

He made a map of the mountain and gave each boy a copy to study. Anthony referred to his map as his 'Go-To for Going To.' They met as a group to discuss the best path to the summit and back home again. During that meeting, several trail options were considered. They were all reasonable possibilities.

"It is a big mountain; there is no one direct path to the top," said Nate.

Each of the boys had different ideas. Any decisions were going to involve compromise with the others.

The four boys were basing their opinions on intuition, given that none had ever done anything like that before. After a lengthy debate, someone had to make the final call, deciding the primary route for the first-time explorers.

Brandon had sat quietly listening to the others. He was the voice of experience as he had traveled to the summit of Majestic Mountain on multiple occasions. He explained to the boys that many of their opinions and intuition were valid, but sometimes intuition combined with lots of experience helps make a better choice.

Brandon laid out the route, considering the others' inputs and preferences. Everyone liked Brandon. Instead of telling the group which way to go, he involved them in the decision-making. This way, they all knew they had been heard. Brandon made the final decisions on the route only after everyone's input was considered. The boys were all just fine with the direction he laid out for them.

Over the next two weeks, the gang gathered all the supplies they would need for the trip. Kim and Lucia pitched in, offering invaluable assistance in locating the more obscure items they would need to take with them, such as lightweight eating utensils and insect repellent.

Victor said, "I don't think any of us realized how much preparation was required when we decided to do this. We need everything from sleeping bags to trash bags."

Phillip had a good idea. He suggested, "You should plan to use only one person's cell phone each day while keeping the others turned off so you can cycle through them individually. This way, you will never use up your joint battery capacity and be without a phone."

Something important had been on Nate's mind since the day at the barbeque when he and his friends decided to make this journey. He was wondering, *How might we all get along over the three-day trip? We will need to stick together and help each other out. If someone goes against another, it could ruin the trip for everyone.*

He realized that their long-term friendship was on the line with this trip. It would be a terrible thing if that were jeopardized in any way. This nagging issue frequently came to Nate's mind, but he could never really put the pieces together.

Nate recognized that sometimes, when he had a lot on his mind like this, giving himself a little quiet time to reflect was good. As strange as it sounds, he was able to identify times when his brain seemed to be in 'execution mode.'

What he came to understand about himself is that there were times when he just wanted to get things done. He learned through experience that these times were usually good for making a list, prioritizing it, and working through the tasks.

There were other times, however, that were a bit more obscure but equally important. These were times when his brain's subconscious almost seemed to take over his thoughts. New concepts would come pouring out like water gushing from an underground spring.

This would generally happen after he had been thinking about the same thing, off and on, for some time. When he recognized these opportunities, he always tried to pull himself away from all distractions. Usually, light physical activity helped him sort things out in this heightened creative state. Sometimes, he would walk or ride his bike along the Wandering River to help inspire the creative process.

The Wandering River meandered through a gorge from the top of Majestic Mountain, then down through Sharefield. It was a beautiful sight.

Nate was unsure why simple repetitive exercises helped him solve problems, but they usually did. During these unpredictable bursts of creativity, new insights about reoccurring thoughts became more evident to him, as if his brain sorted them out in the background. He always made a point of keeping a quick record of them. Some fleeting thoughts were with him for only a few seconds and were easy to forget or dismiss.

In the case of his upcoming adventure, he wanted to figure out how he and his friends could manage three days without the comforts of cooked food and warm beds. This concern had been on his mind since he and his friends decided to attempt this journey that day at the barbecue. Now, almost out of nowhere, things started making sense to him.

After dinner that evening, he took a walk through Sharefield Park. Anthony referred to the park as 'Squirrelly Square' because of all the squirrels and acorn-rich oak trees that adorned the area.

It was only five minutes from Nate's house. As he walked, he envisioned himself alongside his friends, each with unique personalities, strengths, and weaknesses, surviving on Majestic Mountain.

Before that walk, he had an intermittent nagging concern that someone might get upset and ruin their trip. By the time he returned from that walk, just before dark, he had a list of things in his head that he quickly wrote down and would ask everyone to agree to.

Nate was confident that this set of recommendations would help ensure everyone would have a peaceful journey and that their lasting friendships would be preserved.

His list included several important suggestions. He thought it was necessary to make relevant decisions by voting in a democratic process. If he agreed, Dion could lead the group and make the call in case of a tie vote.

No criticism would be allowed when a mistake was made. Nate had come to view mistakes as learning opportunities that often led to a better outcome. He would ask everyone to agree to live in the moment, not the past or present, and accept the current situation, whatever it was.

He realized they would all need to always remain aware of their surroundings and the possibility of danger. Finally, he discovered the value of play, the importance of celebrating individuality, and the utmost requirement to respect each other. He was rather proud of this list.

He thought, *We are about to embark on a perilous journey, so we need to be prepared for everything.*

At Nate's suggestion, the boys met back in the park the next day, where he presented his list of conditions to his friends. Everyone wholeheartedly agreed—they were all in this together. Each of them, for their own reasons, wanted this adventure to be a huge success.

Victor commented, "We have a common goal and understand how to achieve it well before we start. This is exactly how it should be."

Nate nodded, "Yes, it will keep us all moving in the same direction."

Anthony interjected, "Absolutely, we are going up before we come back down. Got it."

"Remember, it matters how we get there," said Nate.

Carrying enough food for three days was another primary consideration.

"We all like different things but can only carry so much," Victor said. "We should all agree not to rely on cooking over an open fire, even though we may make a campfire on suitable evenings for comfort and fun."

Victor did a little research to find out what hikers typically take with them when they plan to be on the trail for days at a time and don't want to deal with cooking hot meals. He found all sorts of recipes on the internet.

"Admittedly, they do not all sound appetizing," he told the others. "These foods are certainly not what we're used to eating. However," he continued, "trying new things will be a part of the experience and worth any slight discomfort. After all, we have the chance to explore the mountain like real pioneers."

Phillip knew a lot about surviving on the mountain. He and Brandon had already earned the boys' respect with their valuable advice for this trip, so the young ones listened when he suggested, "Take lots of tortilla shells and put all sorts of food inside them. They are very versatile," he said, "and don't require refrigeration."

Thanks to Phillip's advice and Victor's internet research, they devised a good list of foods to take.

The menu would include a combination of dried fruits and nuts, beef jerky, apples, soup mix, peanut butter, oats, macaroni and cheese, crackers, cereal, and, of course, tortilla wraps. Anthony referred to this enticing menu as their 'Snack Stack.'

With so much packed, they at least wouldn't go hungry. Fortunately, everyone liked energy bars and planned to take plenty of them. Anthony called them 'Foil Food' because, well, isn't it obvious?

The boys anticipated that the excursion would take three days. To be safe, they planned to carry enough food for a couple of extra days. "You never know what might happen up there," said Dion.

Brandon and Phillip told them there should be plenty of fresh water on the mountain from all the underground springs that rise to the surface along the various trails.

"These springs create a natural drinking fountain," said Brandon. "Although the water may taste a little different."

In Anthony's terms, they would each bring a water bottle or an 'H2O Joe,' which they could refill at each stop.

In addition to all the food, they were packing eating utensils, bowls, a thermometer, a can opener, trash bags, flashlights, lighters, jackets, and an old-fashioned compass just for fun.

Dion said, "I will take my trusty compass, like the one used in our school play."

Kim and Lucia helped them assemble a complete set of supplies for the journey. Their backpacks would be overstuffed and rather heavy, especially at the beginning of the trip.

Initially, they considered taking turns carrying a tent large enough for the four of them. However, they scratched that plan in favor of each carrying a light nylon personal tent so that no one would be burdened with the weight of the much larger version.

Victor kept track of the combined list of items from each friend. He told them, "Things were getting out of hand. There was no way we could carry everything we assembled!"

One afternoon, he sat on his front porch and proceeded to make the journey up Majestic Mountain in his mind's eye. He tried to imagine every detail over the several-day excursion. He meticulously compared his mind's vision of the trip with the items being considered.

By doing so, he could eliminate a lot of the baggage that sounded like a good idea but would probably not be necessary. After several trials, he filled his backpack entirely and perfectly with only the most essential items. The rest of the boys all followed his well-thought-out example.

Dion remarked, "Victor, you are a genius."

Victor replied, pleased with himself, "A little thoughtful planning makes a huge difference."

The gang loaded their backpacks for practice and walked around Sharefield for a couple of hours each day the week before the journey. It was a way of getting in shape and convincing themselves they could make the trip up the mountain. Lucia and Kim usually accompanied them for exercise and moral support. These walks improved the boy's confidence and were a lot of fun for all.

The whole town knew the boys planned to climb Majestic Mountain. As they walked around the neighborhood, they got lots of encouragement and good wishes from the locals. Each day, as they walked past the outdoor equipment store, the owner threw them all a candy bar.

Nate yelled, "Thanks, buddy!"

The old man replied, "I wish I could go along with you."

Dion gave him a high five.

It was a great feeling to know they had everyone's support. Nate put it best when he said, "We are about to be a part of something bigger than ourselves. None of us would attempt this trip alone, but we have a sense of security together. We know that we can rely on each other." The others all agreed.

Dion said, "You got that right."

Dion was still holding on to the key he had found behind the waterfall at the base of the mountain. He considered taking it on the journey as a good luck charm but decided against it. There would be no need for it there, and besides, he was not very superstitious.

He had not told anyone about the key yet. He knew he had in his possession something extraordinary and was trying to understand its significance before he revealed it to the rest of the gang. It needed an explanation.

It indeed was much more than a coincidence that he found this key in the first place. He had a feeling that something would eventually happen that would reveal the purpose of this key to him.

The boys planned to start their journey on the third Tuesday of summer vacation. The weather forecast for the remainder of that week was perfect, with no rain in sight.

This was fortunate because it had been raining heavily the entire week before. During that last week, the boys practiced using umbrellas to walk backpacks around town in the rain. They did not plan to take them on their journey because of the extra weight, but they considered it good training to carry them along on their practice runs around town in the pouring rain.

As the day approached, the boys continued to make last-minute preparations. Brandon and Phillip pulled their gear together quickly and helped the others.

The night before they were to start their adventure, the gang had a wonderful meal prepared by Kim, Lucia, and their families. Kim and Lucia both had mixed emotions about the boys' adventure. On one hand they wanted them to succeed and enjoy the satisfaction of a significant accomplishment. On the other, they felt concern for their safety. They could not imagine how they would feel if something were to go wrong.

The boys went to bed early that night, grateful for the opportunity to explore the many wonders of Majestic Mountain.

Kim and Lucia planned to track their progress through GPS. They downloaded an app on their phones, allowing them to locate the boys' phones so they would know their location throughout the journey. Although the girls would be tracking them, the gang agreed not to call each other back and forth.

After all, this trip was a show of independence and resiliency. The boys wanted to climb the mountain on their own.

5

MAJESTIC MOUNTAIN: THE FIRST MORNING

Everyone agreed to meet at the mountain base at seven sharp on Tuesday morning. Nate woke up at 5:15 a.m. and could not go back to sleep.

As he lay in bed, he anticipated the journey and all the possible new experiences it might bring him. It was a bit overwhelming. He was flush with adrenaline for what he was about to undertake. Later, he discovered that the rest of the group felt the same way. He realized that visualizing the event beforehand helped calm his nerves and prepared him for what was coming.

Nate understood that by living through the event in advance, he would remember things he might have forgotten. It just made him feel more prepared. He had previously described to Kim similar circumstances of living through an experience in his mind's eye before the actual event. Like he did just before they went on stage for their school theater performance. She told him that she does the same thing in her softball games each time before she steps up to the plate. "It must be working," she said. "I have the best batting average on our team."

The gang was all at the base of the mountain on time, except for Victor. He was running ten minutes late. He had forgotten the brownies his mother made for the boys the night before, so he returned home to get them.

Victor thought, *I would rather be late than miss out on those brownies.*

When he arrived and told the others why he was delayed, they all agreed that he had done the right thing.

Dion said, "We will be on the mountain for days. A ten-minute delay for your mom's brownies is a worthy tradeoff."

Brandon and Phillip were also there at the start of the journey. Together, they reviewed the main route and the alternate one for one last time in case of a problem. At seven-forty-five, the boys said goodbye to Brandon and Phillip and embarked on their journey.

It seemed strange to them as they walked away from the security of their homes and families for the first time. None of the boys had really been away from home much before. Brandon and Phillip were very supportive, telling them to have an epic adventure.

As they left alone, they had never felt so much freedom—along with a little healthy fear to go along with it. Dion discovered for the first time that having a little fear can be a tremendous incentive to do extraordinary things that one normally would not consider. He told the others, "I am a little scared of the unknown but extremely motivated to prove that we can do this."

Victor replied, "It's just a stroll around town, only uphill." He did not believe it himself, but it sounded comforting to him and the rest of the gang.

As they started along the trail, Dion reviewed with the others the conditions for the expedition that they had all agreed to before they left. Nate was proud that he had figured much of this out on his own and that the others decided to stick with it.

Nate was thinking, *Already, my backpack is feeling heavy.'*

He would get used to it, he hoped. After all, he and the other boys had carried their backpacks around the neighborhood every day last week as training. By the end of that week, each of them felt confident they could make this journey, at least from a physical conditioning perspective.

Still, Nate's shoulder was hurting a bit. Maybe it was because, this time, they walked on the uneven trail rather than the sidewalk.

Nate grimaced, "Okay, which of you stuffed a lead burrito in my pack?"

Anthony sighed, "It is with a heavy tortilla wrap that I tell you to carry on."

About an hour after they left, they came to the same waterfall their class had visited on their field trip the last week of school. The waterfall was particularly scenic that day, with tons of water rushing over the cliff into the lagoon below from all the rain the week before. The boys sat their backpacks down for a brief rest. They were all laughing and playing around.

Anthony splashed Nate with water, then ran down the trail. Nate caught up with him and dragged him back. Then they all joined in and threw him into the shallow stream off to the side of the waterfall.

Now underway, the boys were celebrating the start of their three-day journey and anticipating the excitement of the adventure. That is all except for Dion. He seemed uncharacteristically quiet. He was thinking about the key he had found at this waterfall just a few weeks before.

Keeping a secret like that wasn't easy, but he wanted to understand more about the key's purpose before sharing it. Dion walked behind the waterfall, where he had stood for the class photo. Victor noticed him. He seemed to be looking into the darkness behind him.

"Hey, Dion!" Victor yelled at him. "What are you doing? Did you lose something back there?"

Everyone laughed as Dion returned from behind the waterfall. He did not take it as a joke. His face was solemn, and his eyes were furrowed in deep concentration.

"I think this journey up the mountain is going to be more than just a couple of days of casual hiking," he said.

Not knowing what to make of the comment, the boys grabbed their gear, continued along the mountain's base, and began the uphill journey. They stopped for lunch to eat the hot dogs and chips they had packed that morning. Everyone knew this would be the last meal they would eat for a few days that was not dried and preserved. While eating, Dion called Brandon and Phillip to tell them all was well. The boys checked their map and confirmed their next destination was a bridge across the Wandering River that feeds the waterfall below.

The river was about an hour away. As they walked toward the bridge, they had to make their way through mud on the trail from all the rain that had fallen just days before. They could hear gushing water as they approached the bridge around the bend. It was not the same intensity as the sound they heard when approaching the waterfall; it was more like a deep, mild roar. The boys all looked at each other with concern and confusion. As they came around the bend, they saw the bridge had flooded!

Water was rushing over the top of it with such violent raging turbulence that it was reflecting white water lathering as it passed. The bridge had been built at the narrowest point of the Wandering River. The water had to funnel between the two large boulders over which the bridge had been constructed.

"Wow!" Anthony said. "The Wandering River has just turned wild, like a tiger about to pounce on its prey."

Nate agreed. "Just standing here at the edge of it feels treacherous."

Downstream of the bridge was a vast lake formed where the water went perfectly still. This was the point where the map split between the primary path and the backup route. The primary path was preferred because it was intended to be a much shorter climb up to the top, although quite a bit more challenging.

The backup route took the boys down part of the mountain, across the river at a lower point, and then back up on the opposite side, the same path they would be descending from. The downhill hike was considerably more straightforward and was expected to take only a day or so. The boys knew the expedition would be far less challenging if they went up that same side.

Dion said, "Let's take a vote to determine if we turn back and detour around the mountain on the alternate route." No one was particularly in favor of that option.

Nate said, "As for myself, I feel like we would be giving up too soon and not facing this mountain head-on. We can't let this flooded bridge stop us so soon on our journey."

The feeling among the others was unanimous. The boys decided to press forward on the primary route if they could find any possible way. That meant they had to figure out how to get to the other side of all that water. Attempting to cross the bridge was out of the question; the water rushing through the narrow passageway was moving so fast that it would surely sweep them against the rocks on either side. Crossing the lake was their only option.

"Why don't we build ourselves a boat and paddle across?" Anthony suggested.

Everyone laughed at first, but Anthony, who was usually joking, didn't have his signature smirk on his face. He explained they could find some branches in the forest and strap them together with vines, just like they did in the olden days.

Victor said, "Well, it seems like an idea worth considering."

Dion added, "Let's see what we can come up with."

The boys started looking around for branches in the nearby woods. They split up so that they could cover more ground.

Victor found a sizable log that he could not move by himself, Dion found a few branches, Anthony found two smaller logs, and Nate located some vines and tall weeds they might be able to use to tie things together.

Victor asked Nate, "Can you help me drag this hefty log down to the lake. It might be useful to us." Nate looked at the log. It was the entire trunk of a tree about as tall as the boys themselves.

"This thing is even heavier than it looks," his lips thinned as he replied.

Though, together the two boys were able to roll it downhill to the shore along with everything else the others were able to scrounge up from the local area.

With all the wood they could find in front of them, they set about trying to figure out how to make a raft with it. Dion haphazardly tied a couple of the sticks together with vines. They did not hold together well.

It wasn't long before everyone realized this idea would not work. They did not have enough branches, and even if they could find more, none of the boys felt comfortable connecting the branches together into a worthy vessel they could ride upon.

"Why don't we try to swim across the lake?" Dion suggested.

Anthony was not a very good swimmer and immediately objected to that idea.

"Are you kidding? This is not the Olympics. I don't think I can make it halfway with all the weight of my backpack."

"You bring up a good point," Victor said. "All of our supplies would get soaking wet, and we may lose part of our food supply. I'm not so sure that's a good idea."

* * *

Kim and Lucia watched the boys' progress by tracking Anthony's phone on the first day as planned. They knew they had stopped at the bridge over the Wandering River.

Kim remarked, "They probably stopped at the bridge to enjoy the scenery and take a rest. It's about their lunch time."

There was no way they could know what was really going on.

Kim was experiencing a bit of a dilemma of her own. Ever since the theater production where she felt some strange connection when she picked up the mysterious key balanced perfectly on edge, she wanted to know more about that production. The unknown author who wrote *The Script* was said to be local. She was becoming obsessed with figuring out just who it was.

She commented to Lucia, "Who do you suppose wrote *The Script*? It has really been bothering me. Do you have any ideas on how we might find out?"

Lucia replied, "Well we could ask around town everywhere we go. You never know, sometimes one connection leads to another and another. Maybe we will discover some useful information that way."

"That sounds like a good idea, Lucia."

* * *

Finally, out of frustration, Nate decided to wade into the water. It was cold, and his feet were sticking in the thick, slimy mud, but to his surprise, the water was only waist deep.

"Hey, maybe we can just walk across," he said.

Dion thought for a moment and then came up with an idea.

"If we each take one of the longer branches we found, maybe we can use them to help us cross. We can each hold a stick and push it through the water to the bottom, always one foot in front of us, so we will know the water's depth before taking the next step."

"That sounds safe enough to me," agreed Victor, "but I am still worried about keeping our food and phones dry."

Dion looked at the remaining wood they had collected.

"Maybe we can take the big log and attach a couple of smaller logs to it," he tried to explain.

When his friends kept quiet, he continued. "By putting one on each side, using the vines, we can make a sort of catamaran with the big log in the center. It should be stable. We can push it across the lake as we walk beside it. We'll put our cell phones on the raft and maybe some food not in sealed containers. If the water gets higher in the middle of the lake—say, up to our shoulders—we can still cross and let the items in our backpacks dry out on the other side. Then we can continue our journey from there."

"That sounds like a plan," Nate said. "I'm in favor of the idea."

Victor and Anthony also thought protecting the phones on a makeshift raft would be a good idea, even if they could not be on top of it themselves. However, Anthony was still apprehensive about crossing the lake by walking with just a branch before him.

"What if the water gets too deep?" he asked.

Dion said, "Let's walk in a single file. I will lead, and Anthony can walk between Victor and Nate, who can be at the back of the line. If the water gets too deep in the center, I will know first, and we can turn around before it's too late."

The modified catamaran went together quickly. Fortunately, the big log still had branches that extended out on each side, so all the boys had to do was secure the outrigger logs to those branches, making the main log stable. The boys slid the raft into the water for a test. It floated perfectly! Everyone cheered.

"It looks like we have a Cell Boat," Anthony said.

Dion took the mesh bag of phones and added to it whatever food had already been opened or was not sealed. He positioned the bag on top of the center log.

"Let's cross this lake," he said.

It was easygoing for the first one-third of the way across. Then, just as Dion had predicted, the water started to get deeper toward the middle. Each of the boys carefully placed their branches in front of their feet with each step they took. Their backpacks were half underwater.

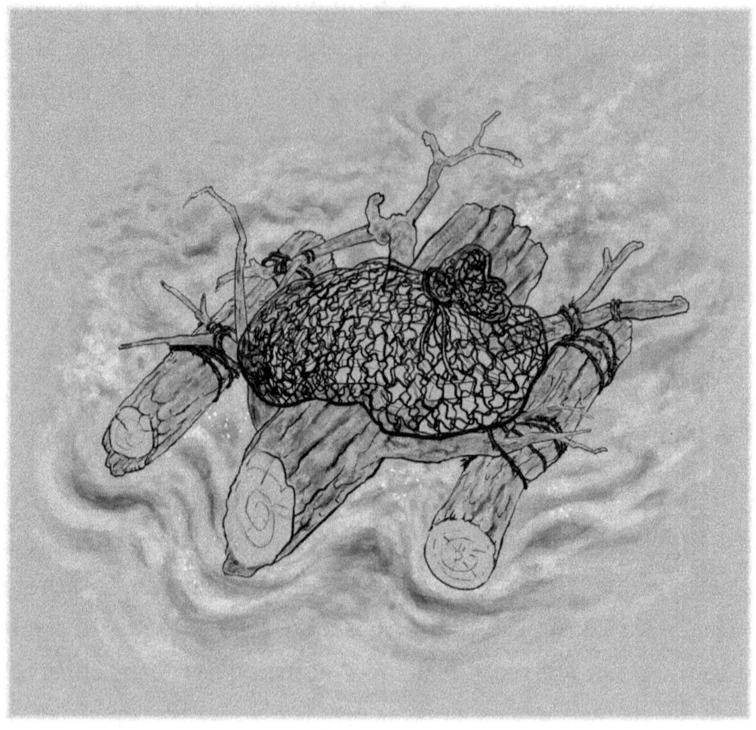

Anthony looked worried. "I can feel the water seeping between my back and my backpack."

They had put their tents in the bottoms of their backpacks before entering the lake, figuring it would not hurt them if they got wet. The catamaran raft was holding up very well. The valued cargo on top was safe and dry. As they approached the far side, the water became shallower again. Everyone sensed that they could make it to the shore with ease.

About that time, Dion realized they had been so focused on getting across the lake that they had forgotten to check in with Brandon and Phillip. "They are probably not overly concerned, but I guess they are waiting on us," he said. "As soon as we make it safely to the far side of the lake, we should call them."

Dion was almost there, only about twenty feet from the edge. The raft was just behind him, in front of Victor. Suddenly, a tree at the edge of the water, which was leaning slightly into the lake due to the erosion of the soil around the lake over the past week, came crashing into the water. It barely missed Dion—and the raft.

"Hey, watch out!" screamed Anthony.

"Wow, that was close!" Dion breathed.

Just then, a large wave created by the tree pouncing into the water rolled over everyone and soaked their backpacks up to their shoulders. The raft tipped and swayed as the lake water came over the top of one of the smaller outboard logs. Suddenly, the mesh bag with the phones in it slid into the turbulent swirl.

"Oh no!" yelled Victor, jumping ahead as fast as possible to retrieve the bag.

The falling tree created an underwater current that grabbed the bag and pulled it under, almost like the attraction of a magnet pulling against another toward the bottom. A vacuum force from water displaced by the tree had swallowed the bag in its entirety. By the time Victor was able to grab it from under the surface of the water, everything in it was completely soaked. In the process, Victor's shirt caught one of the logs and ripped down the side.

The boys quickly made their way to the shore. Victor carried the waterlogged bag over his head, with water still running out the sides. As soon as they climbed up the bank, Victor opened the partially torn mesh bag and pulled the phones out one by one.

"This is not looking good," he winced.

Only Anthony's phone had been turned on, thanks to the group's strategy to use them one at a time. The home screen lit up, but Anthony could not get it to go online or make any calls.

His phone was silver. He called it 'The Long Ranger,' but it was not today. Dion quickly turned his phone on but could not get a signal or any response either. In a state of panic, Nate and Victor also turned on and tried to make a call with their dripping-wet phones. None of them seemed to work. Their phones were as blank as Dion's.

Nate remarked, "I guess we should have waited until our phones dried out before trying to turn them on."

Dion agreed. "Better late than never. Let's ensure they are all off and hope for the best."

Now, they had another decision to make. Should they head back across the lake, abandoning their mission to climb the mountain?

"Let's forge ahead and hope our phones start to work once they dry out," Nate suggested.

"I think it would be best if we just wait here and see if one of our phones will work after they dry," Victor said. "Anthony's phone is lighting up; we can see his home screen. Maybe it will be okay in a short while."

"Even if we put Anthony's phone directly in the sun, it might take the rest of the day for it to dry," Dion said. "Besides, we are all wet, and the mosquitoes are swarming us like a gourmet dinner at a five-star restaurant. Do you really want to spend the rest of the afternoon here?"

"You have a point," said Anthony. "I don't want to just sit here and wait on the Long Ranger to giddy up."

Nate answered, "But I don't want to just give up and go home, either."

"Brandon and Phillip will probably catch up with us sometime during the day," noted Dion.

Victor shook his head. He remembered Dion feeling at the beginning of the trip that this would be more than a simple hike up the mountain.

He said, "I'm still not sure we should just go off without communicating with Brandon and Phillip first."

The other boys, particularly Dion, were much less concerned about contacting Brandon and Phillip. They were confident in the decision to press on, and so they did.

"Come on, Victor, let's go!" Dion yelled.

Victor quickly pulled another shirt from his backpack and put it on. In his haste, he left the old shirt on the ground next to where the tree had fallen into the lake.

6

MAJESTIC MOUNTAIN: DAY ONE

As it turned out, Anthony's phone was surprisingly still broadcasting its GPS signal. Kim and Lucia could see the boys were on the move again, continuing their journey up the mountain on the primary path as planned. The girls were relieved to know that the journey had resumed once again.

Kim was still thinking about the author of and how she might figure out who it was. Lucia had said that she needed to network around town, but she did not know a lot of the adults outside of her friends' parents, who she did not consider to be likely authors. Then she remembered walking through town with the gang prior to the boy's trip. The old man at the outdoor supply store was particularly friendly. She decided to pay him a visit that afternoon to see if he had any information that might lead her to the author. Lucia agreed to go with her for moral support.

As the two girls walked into the store, the old man recognized them right away.

He said, "Hello, young ladies. What brings you in today?"

Before Kim could answer, he asked "How are the boys doing out there on the mountain?"

Lucia replied, "We think they are fine. We are tracking them on GPS.

The store owner looked concerned.

Kim replied, "We agreed not to be in constant contact. As you know, Brandon and Phillip are out there with them. We are sure they're fine."

The old man nodded, saying "Just be aware that there are a lot of dead spots out there on that mountain where internet reception is spotty at best. They are probably having the time of their lives but don't be alarmed if you lose track of them from time to time."

To which Kim replied, thank you for your reassurance and advice, we cannot help but worry a little bit. Actually, we stopped in to speak with you for a different reason."

"Oh, what is that?"

We know that you have dealings with a lot of people around town through sales here at your store. Have you possibly come across anyone who you believe could have been the author of our last year's school play? We understand it was an unknown local writer."

The old man chuckled and said, "No one has come in here to buy outdoor equipment claiming to be an author."

Lucia chimed in, "Perhaps not, but has anyone said anything, or left you suspicious in any way that may lead us to an answer."

The owner thought for a moment then said, "Well there was one person who came in here a few months ago looking for a compass. I could not figure out why. This person did not appear to fit the profile of someone ready to make use of it in the outdoors."

'What do you mean by that?" asked Kim.

"I make it a point not to disclose details of my customers. People come in here buying all sorts of things. I do not ask questions. It is really none of my business, but I will tell you that the situation just felt strange to me."

Lucia asked, "Did this person buy the compass?"

"Yes, and I still have a couple of them in stock." He walked over to a shelf and picked up a gold-colored compass and held it up for the girls to see.

"It was this model, I believe."

Kim recognized it right away, saying to Lucia, "That is just like the one used in our play."

The old man said, "Well, I hope the boys have a great time out there on Majestic Mountain and make it home safely. Please let me know how it all turns out."

Kim and Lucia thanked the store owner and went on their way.

As they walked home, Kim asked, "What do you suppose the old man meant when he said the person who purchased the compass did not appear ready to make use of it."

Lucia replied, "It's hard to say, he sees outdoor enthusiasts every day. I guess this person just did not fit the profile."

* * *

Just after the boys lost sight of the lake, Brandon and Phillip reached the flooded bridge. They immediately tried to call Anthony's phone, but there was no answer.

Looking at the vast lake that had risen into the field downstream of the bridge, they assumed they must have decided to take the alternate route.

It was the only logical conclusion. They could not even imagine the boys would have attempted to cross the lake without a boat, especially knowing Anthony could not swim well. Brandon and Phillip picked up their pace and started on the alternate path that would take them around to the other side of the mountain.

In the meantime, the four were pressing forward on the primary path. They tied their cell phones to the tops of their backpacks so they would be exposed to the sun whenever they were not shaded by the tree-lined path they traveled.

"Maybe it would be a good idea to stop every half hour and see if our phones are working," said Victor.

After the first half hour, Nate tried to turn his on. "The screen is still blank," he reported.

The phones were still so wet that Victor and Dion decided not to try theirs. Anthony's phone was lit up, but there was no change; it was just a nonresponsive home screen. They continued to press onward.

Meanwhile, Brandon and Phillip had been trying to call the boys. They were confused about why they had not yet caught up with them on the alternate path.

All the while, Kim and Lucia could see their friends making progress through their tracking app. Anthony's phone was still transmitting the GPS signal.

Dion's map showed that the gang was approaching Camp Y Knot, an abandoned Boy Scout camp. It got its name from an old white oak tree on the campsite. That tree had a twisted trunk and a large knot right where it split into two large branches. It was a couple of hundred years old and still standing.

Victor said as they approached it, "Wow, the base of this tree trunk is as wide as I am tall."

Everyone marveled at nature's masterpiece standing before them and thought about all the history that old tree must have lived through.

"It probably started to grow around the time the early settlers first explored this land," Anthony said. "It may very well have served as cover during the Civil War. I think we should name it 'The Tree of Knowledge.' I bet it has many secrets in its wood grain from all its history over the past hundreds of years."

Through the ages, some of the bark had peeled off the back side of its massive trunk.

Victor noticed, "If you stare at the wood grain in the exposed area, you can see what appears to be an image of a bicycle."

It was not obvious, but everyone saw it once Victor pointed it out. That image in the bark further added to the mystique of the age-old tree, now called 'The Tree of Knowledge,' thanks to Anthony.

A freshwater pump at the camp looked like it had been repaired in recent years.

Nate said, "There are old pipes here from an obvious recent repair. Let's see if we can get some water from this well."

He began to push the handle up and down as water started to roll out of the spout. Initially, it was just a trickle but gradually increased to a mighty stream. It was cold and refreshing. The boys filled up their water bottles and rinsed off some of the dirt they had accumulated on the trail.

Dion suggested that everyone try their cell phones again, but they were still not working. The boys were beginning to resign themselves to the idea that these phones may not be useful for the rest of their journey.

That did not really bother them too much. They were together, a tight group of friends who could depend on each other. They each raised their right hands and touched together in the center like a sports team, ready to start a championship game. Besides, in their minds, they expected that Brandon and Phillip would catch up with them soon. They had no inkling that their support, in case of an emergency, was trying to track them down on the alternate route.

After a brief rest, they started into the dense forest, which took them farther up the mountain. Just before entering the tree line, Victor's eyes darted up and saw something strange. The formation of the clouds combined with the outline of the massive white oak tree looked just like the profile of a bear. He laughed and pointed it out to Anthony.

"Check out the bear in the sky!" he yelled.

Anthony raised his arms like he would attack and started chasing Victor around. Everyone laughed.

The forest was covered with a carpet of ground cover foliage, but the path was clear. The cool breeze felt good under the shade of the trees lining the path on both sides. As they walked along, the hikers looked in amazement at both sides of the trail. The ground was covered with a wide variety of plants. The ferns waving in the breeze made the whole atmosphere appear almost mystical. There were birds of many species, large and small, and squirrels scurrying in circles on the ground and up the trees. The forest was alive with a diverse combination of sounds so loud that one had to speak up to be heard.

Then, suddenly, off in the distance between two trees, Dion spotted what looked like a large brown bear. He was startled and screamed, "Bear!"

Everyone laughed, but Dion was not taking any chances. He started running back down the trail. The others knew he was serious and followed him as fast as possible. The boys ran back to the clearing at the edge of Camp Y Knot. They were all winded when they arrived.

As Nate gasped for air, he asked Dion, "How big was it?"

Dion said, "Big enough, I think. If I were that bear and saw me, I might be considering lunch."

Brandon had warned the boys there used to be bears on the mountain, but none had been seen in a couple of years. He told them he thought an encounter with one would be rare. But there they were, faced with having to make their way through the dense forest, knowing that Dion thought he had seen at least one bear large enough to have them for dinner. The suspected bear sighting was creepy, considering that the clouds in the sky, combined with the branches of the Tree of

Knowledge, looked like a bear silhouette just a few minutes before. The image in the clouds was gone now.

"This is spooky strange," said Victor.

"I am not going back into that forest with Cloud Claw, the Billowing Bear," Anthony said.

"The whispering wind has blown him away!" chuckled Nate.

"What we need is a bear defense system," Victor suggested. "Something that will protect us from the grizzly beast."

"What can we come up with that would possibly be strong enough to protect us from a full-grown bear?" asked Anthony.

As Nate thought about it, it occurred to him that they may all be overreacting to the danger.

The whispering wind has blown him away . . . That triggered a thought. Nate remembered reading that bears prefer not to attack humans, and if they are not startled, they will tend to avoid them altogether.

"What we need is a way to make our presence known to the bear so that it will not be startled as we pass by," he explained. "We need to make lots of noise."

Everyone agreed, so they went about trying to figure out how they would continuously make a lot of noise for the next three hours as they walked through the dense forest.

Victor asked, "Why don't we just yell?"

Anthony rolled his eyes and said, "We cannot possibly yell for three hours straight."

"Well, maybe we could sing?" Dion suggested.

"That isn't any better," said Nate. "It's going to tire us out. Trying to walk the trail, which might involve climbing up and down with our heavy backpacks, while trying to sing or yell the entire time does not sound like a good idea."

Victor said, "Why don't we clap our hands instead of singing?" but Dion disagreed.

"A single person clapping would not be very loud. It does not seem practical for all of us to clap together for three hours straight. Besides, we may need our hands to climb."

Nate said, "I have heard that people carry bells into areas where there might be bears and ring them constantly to warn the bears of their presence."

"The only problem is that we don't have a bell," said Dion.

Then he got an idea.

"Why don't we see if we can find a hollow log and hit it with a stick in place of a bell?"

Everyone looked around for such a log for half an hour, but all they could come up with was a short log that was partially hollow on one end. Victor tried banging on it; it just made a thud.

"That will never be loud enough," said Victor. "Or maybe it will be."

"We're not going to take any chances," said Dion.

Nate got an idea. "Maybe we can cover the face of the hollow end of the log, making it into a drum."

"That sounds like a bang-up idea!" cried Anthony.

Dion immediately grabbed his pocketknife and started trying to flatten the top surface of the log so that a drumhead could be stretched over it.

Victor asked the next question.

"Where do we get a drumhead, and how do we tension it over the top of the log?"

"Animal skins are often used for drumheads," Nate said.

The boys had seen a couple of dead animals inside the forest, but none were interested in returning to get one. Besides, even the thought of trying to skin a dead animal and wrap its skin around the log was out of the question. No one was in favor of trying to do something that disgusting.

But they wouldn't give up until they came up with a workable solution. Victor had an idea. He had brought a thin nylon jacket. He pulled it from his backpack and stretched it over the partially hollowed log.

"Now, hit it with a stick," he instructed Dion. He did so, but it made a low bass note that did not ring out loud enough to be helpful.

The boys huffed out disappointed sighs. They were just about out of ideas. They were considering abandoning their journey and returning home.

Dion sighed. "We can probably make it back to the base of the mountain by nightfall."

Everyone sat quietly, considering the devastating outcome of not finishing their long-awaited expedition.

* * *

The girls could see that the boy's progress had once again stalled. They were concerned and wondering what their friends were going through.

"They sure are taking their time. I wonder if there's a problem or if they're just taking it easy," said Kim.

"Considering how excited they were to climb that mountain and their week of practice walking around town with their backpacks, I would suspect they have run into an issue of some sort," Lucia replied.

Kim nodded thoughtfully. "Maybe you are right—let's keep close track of them."

* * *

After pondering for a moment in the quiet of nature, Dion suggested maybe they could make a wind chime.

Nate looked at him like he usually did when Dion had an idea Nate didn't understand. Dion thought of bells and remembered hearing the high-pitched sound of wind chimes on his neighbor's porch. He jumped up and ran toward the water well at the far end of Camp Y Knot.

"Where are you going?" yelled Victor.

Dion picked up one of the old pipes that had been replaced at the water pump and returned it to the gang.

He said, "This pipe might work like a wind chime."

Nate grabbed the stick they were using to hit the nylon jacket drum and started banging on the pipe as Dion held it in place. It made a quiet, high-pitched ringing sound but nothing more.

Victor remembered what Lucia had done at the picnic that day when she solved the problem with the rocket launcher. In her mind, she traveled with the electricity down the wire from the remote launcher to the rocket, where she realized that the wire was too thick to ignite the fuse.

Victor applied the same technique here. In his mind, he went inside the pipe and realized the sound vibrations created by the stick's impact were dampened by Dion's hand.

"Yes, that's the answer!" he exclaimed. "A wind chime pipe hangs from a string that allows the pipe to vibrate freely. Maybe we need to hang the pipe on a string."

Unfortunately, the pipe did not have a hole through it for a string, but it did have a coarse pipe thread on one end.

Dion said, "Let's look around for a vine or some plant we can wrap around the pipe thread so it can hang freely. If we tie the vine around the thread snugly and then cover it with some tree sap, it will hold together. The sap is available here on the trunks of the many pine trees lining the forest." Nate replied, "I see a thin vine growing up the side of a tree from here. Let me go get it. We will give this idea a try."

The vine stem was quite thin, but so was the diameter of the pipe. Trying to wrap it tightly around the pipe caused the vine to split. The tree sap held it in place while they tested it for a couple of minutes, but it was clear it would not hold up for the entire journey through the forest.

The gang was back to thinking they should just head home. Suddenly, Dion jumped up and ran off again. This time, he was headed toward the group of backpacks the boys had removed from their shoulders while they tried to solve the noisemaker problem. He pulled out an extra pair of tennis shoes he had brought with him in case of an emergency and removed one of the shoelaces. He said, "Let's wrap this string tightly into the threads on the end of the pipe and tie it. Nate, put your finger on the first knot to secure it while I tie a double knot and pull it against the first."

Dion pulled on the two ends so hard he nearly broke the shoestring in half.

"There, now hit the pipe with the stick," Dion said.

Nate hit it while Dion held the loose end of the shoelace. The pipe rang out loud and clear. Everyone cheered!

They had their bear-warning device. Now, they could each take turns ringing the pipe as they walked through the woods, feeling confident that any bear nearby would not be startled by their presence.

Making light of the situation, Anthony said, "You did it. Our pipe bell is a bear bell, much lighter than a solid barbell, ringing loud and true because it is hollow. Behind that pied piper, I will follow. With this chime, we should make it through the woods in record time.

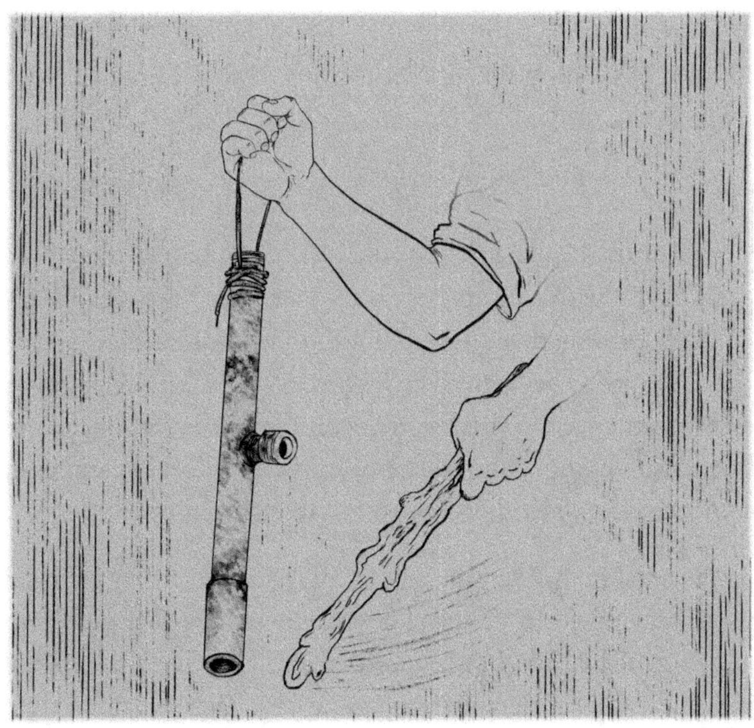

Before heading back into the woods, the boys rang their new pipe bell, hoping that Brandon and Phillip would hear it and send them a signal. They rang and rang and then listened, but there was no response other than from some chirping songbirds who were amused by their bell.

* * *

Brandon and Phillip continued firmly along the trail, which pushed them farther away from the boys. Brandon stopped and tried to call them frequently, but his phone rang without an answer, just like the pipe bell. The older boys were getting more concerned as the afternoon wore on.

* * *

Armed with their makeshift pipe bell, they entered the wood, pounding it with a steady beat as they advanced between the giant trees shading them from the sun. Victor volunteered to take the first turn. They agreed to switch every twenty minutes so none would get too tired banging on the pipe. Anthony could not resist singing along to the beat of the bell. He composed some words as the others joined in for a few choruses.

Advancing through the woods, they saw what they believed to be bear tracks in the mud beside the trail, which put them all on guard for any potential danger. They were all a little jumpy, and the adrenaline was pumping. This was not a time for relaxation, but good fortune smiled upon them. The long hike through the woods was uneventful, much to their relief.

* * *

Back home, the girls could see their friends had resumed their journey. That made them feel much more at ease. In their jubilation, they sent a text to the boys that was never received. Now, suddenly, they were feeling a little anxious.

Lucia said, "Those boys are so focused on their journey that they probably have not even looked at their phones."

Kim agreed. "That's right, no need to be worried at all."

But secretly, they were.

* * *

When the boys reached the other side of the forest, they were all hungry and exhausted. They stopped in a flat, grassy field on the side of the mountain for dinner. The sun was already starting to go down. The journey through the woods at such a heightened level of anxiety drained them of energy far beyond what the task would have normally demanded.

They sat quietly, grateful the woods were behind them. They ate some of their preserved food for dinner. It was not particularly tasty, but they were all happy to have something to eat.

Nate told Victor, "Thanks for planning so well and knowing how to bring extra food in case something unpredictable happened. We still have enough to finish our journey. That is, if everything goes as planned from here on."

After the gang finished eating, they decided to advance up the mountain for one more hour and set up camp for the night. The next hour's walk was relatively easy compared to what the boys had been through earlier in the day. They found a uniquely scenic site to camp that looked out over the valley below.

From the edge of the rocky height in front of their campsite, they could see the rolling farmland and parts of Sharefield. A small stream ran through the bottom of the cliff below. They each set about putting up their tents, unrolling their sleeping bags, and preparing for their first night out in nature.

Anthony said that he was really looking forward to sleeping in his little *'Butt Hut,'* the name he had given to his one-man tent. This was a different feeling than when they pitched a tent in their backyards and slept out with the stars. This was the real thing.

Dion said, "Let's build a fire."

Plenty of dry sticks were around them, and they had brought a lighter from home.

"This is something we need to vote on," Victor said. "There could be some risk of the fire getting out of control if the wind were to pick up."

Everyone agreed and voted in favor of the fire, except for Victor. As tempting as it was, he was concerned something bad might happen. After some discussion, they decided that no one would sleep until the fire was completely out. That way, they could watch it and not let it get out of hand.

"If the wind picks up, we can put out the fire with a pile of dirt that we could prepare before lighting it," Nate suggested.

That made everyone feel at ease, so they grabbed handfuls of rocks and dirt and laid them by the fire they were about to start. They each set their nearly full water bottles in the same area in case they were needed, just to be extra cautious.

Surprisingly, the tracking app remained active, so the girls knew their friends had stopped for the day. It was sundown. Kim turned off the tracking application for the evening. They would sleep well that night knowing the boys' journey was progressing somewhat on schedule, even though they were not able to contact them directly.

Lighting a fire turned out to be a favorable decision. Everyone enjoyed roasting marshmallows and eating them with the brownies Victor's mother had made for them. The gang all felt a huge sense of satisfaction after the day's journey. Even though they had lost their phones and all communication with Brandon and Phillip, they took pride in being on their way up Majestic Mountain.

In their minds, they each thought that Brandon and Phillip would likely catch up soon.

Nate commented, "We might all be together in the morning to continue our journey."

The boys kept a lookout for them, thinking that the fire might be the signal they needed, but Brandon and Phillip never showed up. After dark, the boys put the fire out, and each headed off to their small but comfortable one-person tents.

Once the fire went out, the boys could not help but notice how dark it was up there on the mountain. They each had individual flashlights, but they could not see anything outside that narrow beam of their visual reality.

"The stars in the sky have never looked so bright," Anthony marveled.

Victor said, "I think the number of stars must multiply by three every time I look up."

Anthony, making a joke, chirped, "Well, then quit looking up, or it will be so bright from all the stars that we will not be able to sleep."

It was truly a beautiful sight.

The boys were all so tired from the day's journey that they hardly hit their heads on their makeshift pillows before they were all fast asleep.

Nate woke up in the middle of the night to strange sounds on the mountain. Mixed with the howling wind, which had picked up considerably since they went to sleep, he could hear the screech of a barn owl and the distant cry of coyotes. It bothered him a bit to think of what else might be lurking around in the darkness, but he was so tired that he quickly fell back to sleep. The next thing he knew, it was morning, and everyone was up.

7

MAJESTIC MOUNTAIN:
THE SECOND MORNING

Anthony woke before the others and sat at the cliff's edge, looking down at the stream below. He marveled at the path of the water making its way around the rocks in front of it, attempting to block its forward motion.

He noted that the water always took the path of least resistance around any obstacle. It knew which way to flow.

He thought, *This natural phenomenon might be true in other aspects of nature, just like the electricity flowing through the wire of Dion's rocket launcher. This might be something to remember. Perhaps other things in nature, and even people, do the same thing.*

The boys packed up their tents and ate a breakfast of granola bars, fruit, and juice made from a powdered mix. No longer sleep-deprived, everyone was upbeat and eager to start the second day of their adventure.

Dion said, "I am really puzzled about what might have happened to Brandon and Phillip. I thought for sure they would catch up with us last night."

They each pulled out their cell phones and tried once again to call them, but none of the phones would work.

"I wish these phones were a bit more waterproof," grumbled Nate.

Anthony looked at Nate's light-blue phone and quipped, "You have a phony aqua waterproof phone."

"Yes, your silver long ranger is in the same boat," Nate responded. "Or at least it was until they all fell out."

Dion laughed and said his black phone matched the color of his screen. Ironically, Victor's phone turned on and showed one percent battery life, then randomly flashed *Have a nice day*, before it went blank.

* * *

Brandon and Phillip had scurried on the alternate route to the other side of the mountain, thinking they would surely catch up with the boys if they moved quickly. They did not even stop for dinner. They tried to contact the boys by phone all day yesterday with no success.

Not wanting to alarm their parents and the rest of the town, they decided to wait and see if they could contact the missing hikers the following day.

They planned to split up.

Brandon said, "I will continue to look for them along the alternate path up the mountain."

Phillip replied, "Yeah, that's a good idea. I will backtrack toward the primary trail just in case we somehow missed the boys on that trail yesterday. Or maybe they're planning on taking that path today. Let's stay in touch by phone. Let me know if you come across anything, anything at all, that could lead us to them."

* * *

Kim had an early morning double-header softball game with a rival team that day. Lucia was there to cheer her on. The girls tried to restart the GPS app before going to the ballpark, but there was no signal. They figured the boys had not gotten up and turned on a second phone yet.

Lucia said, "Let's check for a signal after today's baseball games."

* * *

Meanwhile, the boys felt well-rested and prepared to begin their second day on the mountain. The air was cool, adding to their excitement and energy.

They walked briskly for about an hour until they came to a part of the path that was still particularly muddy. More rain had fallen in that area last week than in many years. The boys' feet were heavy with the weight of the mud on their shoes. Victor found a stick and stopped for a moment. He began to clean some of the mud.

Everyone else stopped with him and looked ahead.

"How will we climb the steep hill in front of us in all this mud?" Nate asked. "It's so slippery."

The incline stretched across the trail and as far as the boys could see in both directions.

Then, suddenly, they heard a disturbing rumbling sound. Before they knew it, the mud was rolling down the hillside straight toward them!

It knocked them off their feet, then stopped at a line of trees just behind them. Dion stood up and called out names, one at a time.

"Victor."

"I am here!"

"Nate?"

"I'm okay."

"Anthony."

"I'm a mudslinger."

They were drenched with mud from head to toe and found themselves standing in a slushy mess up to their knees. They backed up behind the tree line to get out of the stuff.

"Wow, that was a close one!" huffed Dion.

The insides of their backpacks were still clean, so they each pulled out a spare T-shirt and wiped their faces to see clearly.

Victor said, "We're lucky to all be alive. Has anyone seen water nearby where we can wash off some of this mud?"

It dried quickly in the summer sun, leaving the boys looking like thick icing on a cake.

Unfortunately, they had not passed a stream since they had started on their way earlier that morning. They decided to put on a spare set of clothes and use only one of several water bottles each to clean themselves up.

They stuffed their muddy clothes into the plastic trash bags Victor made sure that they brought and put them in their backpacks.

Nate said, "Well, I am feeling somewhat back to normal after what could have been a dire catastrophe."

They all nodded.

Now, they had to figure out what to do next. The fallen mud had exposed a rock cliff across the path in both directions. The mud pile at the cliff's bottom made climbing impossible for the boys.

Dion suggested, "Let's walk off the trail to the left along the ridge. Maybe we will find a place where we can scale the cliff. Then we can return to the top side's main trail."

"That sounds like a good plan," said Victor, so they took off to the left of the trail. It seemed to Victor like they were walking a very long way—though it was only the equivalent of a few city blocks—before they came to a section of the cliff where there was less mud at the base. The only problem was that the incline was straight up about fifteen feet with nothing to grab hold of except a large tree that hung over the edge at the very top. The boys stopped to look.

Victor hesitated. "There is no way we will get up that cliff."

"Well, then, let's move on, hoping to find a better spot to scale the cliff," Nate said.

They walked a little farther along the base of the ridge, but it appeared to be getting higher the farther they went.

"Let's return to the first plausible spot we found and try to figure out how to scale the cliff there," Dion suggested.

It looked even more formidable as they reached the location where they had been just a few minutes ago.

Victor asked, "How can we scale a cliff that is straight up fifteen feet with nothing to grab hold of?"

Nate had an idea. "Anthony is the lightest and most athletic among us. Maybe Victor and Dion could help Anthony stand on my shoulders."

"Even then, he would still be several feet from the top of the cliff," Victor said. He paused before adding, "Maybe Anthony could take his belt and loop the end through the buckle to make a lasso and throw it over a branch in the tree at the top while standing on Nate's shoulders."

Everyone agreed that it was a good idea and well worth a try.

Anthony said, "If I can get the belt around a tree branch that overhangs the cliff, I can pull myself up the belt to the top."

"But then what?" Dion asked. "We need to figure out how to get everyone up before we jump into this." He thought for a moment and then suggested, "Once Anthony is on top, we could each throw him our belts, and he could hook them all together to make a rope that would extend down far enough for the rest of us to grab and pull ourselves up to join him."

Victor and Nate were not sure they could climb up a belt rope, but it was their best option, so they decided to go with the plan.

Anthony stood on Nate's shoulders. Victor and Dion were able to steady him.

Nate said, "I feel my feet sinking deeper into the mud."

Anthony tried several times to throw the belt up and loop it over the main branch of the tree, but the belt was too short.

"Give me another belt," said Anthony.

Dion loosened his belt, pulled on it from one end as it snapped through the loops in his pants, then tossed it up to Anthony. He leaned to catch it, almost falling off Nate's shoulders. After he steadied himself, he attached it to his own to make the lasso longer. Anthony tried several times to catch a tree branch with the looped end of the belt. Finally, he snagged a good, strong one extending over the embankment. He pulled on the belt rope from his end, tightening it against the sturdy branch. Then he tested it by pulling on it several times while removing some of his weight from Nate's shoulders.

"It feels solid," he said.

Anthony extended his arms, grabbed hold of the two-belt chain as high as he could, and lifted himself clear off Nate's shoulders. He was hanging there as everyone began to cheer him on. They quickly, almost effortlessly, pulled himself up the belts.

He advanced, moving one hand over the other until he was on top of the cliff, looking down, saying, "I did it! Come on up and join me. The weather up here is fine."

Victor and Nate each threw Anthony their belts. He pulled up the ones hanging from the tree branch and secured the two additional ones to the end. As planned, the four belts extended just far enough for the boys to grasp from the base of the cliff.

Dion said, "I will go first."

He grabbed hold of the end of the belt rope and pulled himself to the top to join Anthony. Next, Nate tried, but his hands kept slipping off the belts about halfway up.

Victor said, "I have an idea." He remembered that he had saved the pipe bell used in the woods to scare off any bears in case they needed it again along the way. He pulled it out of his backpack and threw it up to Dion.

Dion knew exactly what he was thinking and said, "Great idea!"

He pulled the belts up from the top, attached the pipe to the buckle between the lower two belts, and then dropped them back over the cliff's edge.

The pipe served as a handle for Nate to grab hold of and pull himself up. Then, Nate stood on the pipe once he worked up the belts toward the top. It made climbing much easier. He said, "I probably could not have made it up without the aid of that pipe. Thanks, Victor."

Then Dion told Victor, "Just climb up the same way Nate did, using the pipe first as a handhold and then as a step once you get near the top."

Victor started up the lower belt, grabbed the pipe and pulled himself up. As he attempted to go higher, the pipe slipped out of the belt and tumbled to the ground. Victor was hanging there!

His arms began to shake from the stress on his muscles. Victor said in a strained voice, "I'm not going to be able to hold on much longer."

"Let's pull him up," Dion instructed.

So, Dion and Nate grabbed the belt below the tree branch and pulled Victor to safety. They all cheered and gave each other high fives for another significant accomplishment.

Dion lifted the belt rope and undid the loops holding them together. The boys each put their belts back on and realized the pipe bell was the only thing they had lost. All was well as they returned along the top ridge to the main trail.

8

MAJESTIC MOUNTAIN: DAY TWO

By this time, Kim had finished her softball games, with two wins. The first was a no-hitter, thanks to her well-practiced pitching skills. The second game went into an extra inning with a five-to-four victory on an error by the opposing team's second basemen.

After the games, Kim approached Coach Johnson and asked her if she had a couple minutes to spare.

She happily obliged saying, "You played very well today. You are really showing leadership to the rest of the team. What is on your mind?"

Kim's face was flush with embarrassment from the compliment, she composed herself and said, "My question does not have to do with baseball. I know that you attended our theater production of *The Script* at the end of the school year. Do you have any idea who the author was? It is something that has been bothering me."

Coach Johnson replied, "I have no knowledge of this. Admittedly, theater is not my first interest, but if I hear anything related to your question, I will be certain to share it with you."

Kim was satisfied with her response and said, "Thank you I would appreciate it." Then the girls immediately attempted to locate their friends on the mountain through the GPS application again. Strangely, there was no new location information. The GPS signal had not been updated since the night before!

"This doesn't seem right," said Lucia. "Victor was supposed to use his phone today. Perhaps he did not activate the GPS signal."

"Maybe we should wait till tomorrow morning and pick up Nate's phone signal," Kim suggested. "They should be at the top of the mountain by then if all is going according to plan."

"I don't know . . . That doesn't sound like Victor; he is so organized and responsible," said Lucia. "I know we agreed that we were not going to contact the boys on the mountain, but under the circumstances, we should send them a text. One of them should have their phone turned on."

Kim wrote a quick one-line text, "Are you guys okay?" She tapped on 'send,' and it was off.

No response came back. Lucia said, "Maybe they are just in a dead spot with limited or no cell phone reception. The owner of the outdoor supply store warned us of this possibility yesterday. Brandon and Phillip are out there on the mountain with them. They are probably all fine. Let's not overreact at this point."

But Lucia's words did little to comfort the dread rising into their throats.

Kim confessed to Lucia as she opened her purse, "Do you see this locket?"

"Yes," said Lucia, "that is a nice picture of you."

"I considered hiding this inside of Dion's backpack so he would find it on their journey and think about me. I thought it might be distracting at a time when the boys need to concentrate on their mission, so I decided against it. I don't want anything to get in the way of a successful journey."

Lucia replied, "Perhaps you are on his mind anyway."

"That is a nice thought. Maybe Anthony is joking around as usual and had mentioned you a time or two, as well."

* * *

The boys were all hungry as they returned to the main trail. It was already well past lunchtime, so they ate there before continuing their journey.

Victor had brought a special treat from home: preserved peaches that he wanted to share with everyone. The peaches were in a sealed mason jar that he had carried all this distance just for a moment like this one. He pulled the large jar out of his backpack and surprised everyone. Then he tried to open it. It had been sealed for a long time. The lid was large and hard to grasp. He tried several times but could not get the lid off. Each boy took a turn, but that lid was sealed on the jar like a concrete mortar joint between two bricks.

"Why don't we try hitting the lid lightly with the blunt end of my pocketknife?" Dion suggested.

Victor gave that a try. As he tapped around the edges of the jar, it made a thumping sound as mouths began to water. After going around the lid several times, Victor tried again to open the jar, but it would not budge. He did not want to hit the lid so hard that it might shatter the glass jar. "This is really discouraging," he mumbled.

The boys began to pull out other dry snacks from their backpacks. Victor was thinking back over some of the trip's adventures as he ate a granola bar and drank water with powdered cherry flavoring. He thought how lucky they were to have found the pipe at the abandoned well at Camp Y Knot. Then he remembered the image of a bicycle that he saw in the exposed wood grain of the giant white oak Tree of Knowledge.

Suddenly, an idea came to him. He thought, *A bicycle crank has gear teeth, which drive the chain to turn the back wheel as one pedal's forward.*

He realized that the lid to the preserved peaches was serrated, not unlike the gear of a bicycle crank. He thought that if he could find another surface that would wrap around the lid and mesh with its serrated edge like the chain on a bicycle, he could turn the lid and open the jar.

Victor mentioned this idea to everyone else. His friends were all intrigued with the concept and extremely motivated to open that jar as they could see the delicious peaches floating inside. Victor started looking around for something that might fit against the lid of the peach jar.

Then Dion laughed, saying, "The answer might be on your head."

"Yes," Victor said, "I know it is close in my head, but I cannot think of what it might be."

"No," Dion said, "maybe it is *on* your head. Look at your hat!"

Victor was wearing his favorite corduroy baseball hat. Confused, he reached up and pulled the cap off his head. Sure enough, the spacing in the lined corduroy fabric closely matched the serrations surrounding the canning jar lid.

"Whoa!" said Victor, grinning. "Now that's what I call teamwork."

Victor turned his hat upside down over the jar and held it tightly against the lid with his left hand. Then, with his right hand, he pushed on the bill of his hat.

The lid slowly began to turn, then went *POP!* as it spun off the top of the jar. Everyone cheered.

Victor said, "I am not sure how we managed to figure this out, but I am sure glad we did."

Then, he gave Dion a high five. Anthony was impressed. "The way you guys got the lid off that jar was absolutely uncanny."

Victor split the jar up equally among the four of them. Everyone voiced their approval and slurped down the peaches in a matter of minutes before the flies in the area could swarm the sweet nectar. The boys were not supposed to bring glass jars on this trip, but no one was complaining.

After lunch, they gathered their belongings and started up the trail. This section was a particularly steep incline. Progress was slow throughout the hot afternoon, and they huffed and puffed all the way.

* * *

In the meantime, Brandon was making his way up the back of the mountain as Phillip retraced his steps toward the point where the path split in two directions. They figured they would surely catch up with the boys sometime in the afternoon. As the day wore on, they began to change their minds.

Brandon and Phillip, who were in constant contact, decided to alert the townspeople along with the boys' parents by the end of the day. Phillip returned to where the trail split and gave Brandon another call. By then, Brandon was just a couple of hours from the summit of the mountain. Brandon decided to go to the summit before nightfall and camp there.

Phillip would head back down the mountain and inform everyone in Sharefield of the predicament if, by chance, they had not run into the boys before then.

The gang continued their journey, walking uphill directly into the sun. It was intensely bright and burning hot. They started thinking that maybe they should have taken the alternate route to the back of the mountain, but it was too late.

They stopped frequently for water breaks and were getting low on water. The sun was so bright they could hardly see in front of them.

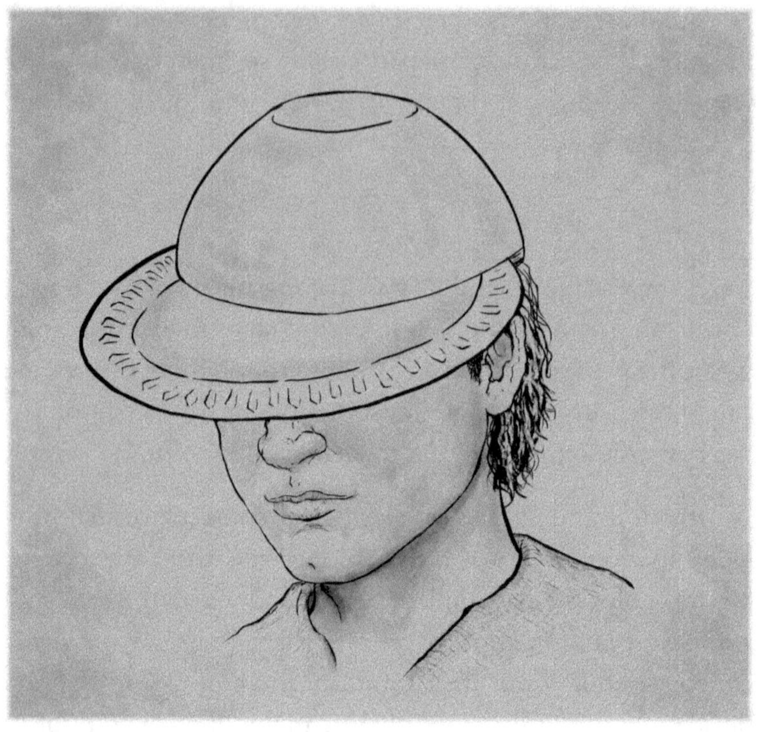

Anthony was looking at Victor's baseball hat, wishing he had one of his own to block the sun. He took a large used Tupperware bowl out of his backpack and cut a hole in the lid, leaving only the rim that attached to the bowl. Then, he cut a similar hole off-center in a paper plate.

Next, he sandwiched the plate between the bowl and the cutout lid, making a hat with a bill formed by the plate. He put it on his head. Everyone laughed at Anthony but had to admit that the makeshift hat served him well. His eyes and the rest of his face were shielded from the sun.

He was grinning from ear to ear in his newfound attire. Only Anthony would be silly enough to do something like that. He said, "My new hat, *Tupper Tough*, works plenty well enough."

As they walked, they came to a path that branched off to the right. Their map said they should take that turn to head north; it would lead to the top of the mountain.

"It looks like it's going in the wrong direction," Nate said. "I think we are headed straight toward the top of the mountain on the path we are on."

A flock of geese flew overhead in their customary 'V' formation. They were pointing straight along the path the boys were already on.

Victor said, "Continuing straight ahead on this path also seems right to me."

Dion wasn't sure. "Let's check the compass."

He pulled out his old-fashioned manual compass, and everyone laughed as they recalled the school play where the compass lit up to show the correct direction.

It was not lighting up today, just reflecting the sun so brightly that the boys could hardly read it.

Dion looked closely and noted, "It's pointing straight ahead, definitely due north. But the map says that we should take the path to our right to go north."

According to the compass, that path pointed to the east. Dion suggested they take a vote. They decided to keep moving straight ahead toward the top of the mountain.

"Look!" said Nate. "We can see the peak from here, off in the distance."

"The compass says north is straight ahead, and the map says to go north," Victor explained, "so that must be the right way, even though the map shows we should be taking the path off to the side."

"Let me get this straight," Anthony remarked, "we are not going off at the right angle because we think it is the wrong direction."

"Yes, Anthony, that is correct."

Soon after taking this straight path, they found a freshwater underground spring that passed through a deep crevasse in the rock. The water looked clear and pure. Dion stuck his hand in it.

"Wow! It's freezing. To be this cold on such a hot day it must have come from an underground spring."

It was late afternoon. Dion said, "Let's stop here and make a fire to boil the water from the spring, just to be sure it is safe to drink. Then we can fill all our water containers." No one disagreed.

Everyone felt like they could use a break after the strenuous hike and hot sun they had endured that day. Nate gathered up some small branches while Dion started a fire in a safe clearing. They only had one metal pot with them, so they had to boil the water in stages, then transfer it to the empty peach jar to cool while starting to boil more. This process took quite a while. Once everyone filled their water bottles, Dion put out the fire.

They decided to go ahead and eat dinner there since everyone was already sitting comfortably, and it was getting late in the day. Dion figured they should plan to hike for another hour or two after dinner and then set up camp for the night.

Dinner that evening was not very exciting. It was lunch all over again, consisting of dried beef jerky in a tortilla, granola, dried fruit bars, and, of course, brownies. The thrill of the hiking adventure was beginning to wear off. The whole group craved warm beds and hot, home-cooked meals.

"Maybe I'm just tired," said Victor, "but this is starting to feel old."

Again, nobody countered.

After they ate, they packed up and started on their way. The alternate path they had taken, which seemed like such a good idea at the time, was now twisting and turning in different directions around the mountain. The boys knew they were near the top, but sometimes, it seemed they were walking in the wrong direction, away from the summit. The wind started to pick up. It was howling through the trees like a ghost from an old horror movie. Perhaps it was the elevation, but it got so strong that the boys could hardly walk forward into it. The fact that they were drained did not help matters. Victor stood still at one point, not knowing if he should push forward or fall backward.

Dion suggested they look for a place to stop for the night, then head for the summit in the morning. The rest of them thought it to be a prudent suggestion. There was just one problem. They could not find a place to hide from the strong and intense forest wind.

Nate said, "The wind is roaring so violently through the trees that I fear a large branch might break loose and fall on us. Several large branches on the ground have already broken off the tops of the towering trees."

"It would be catastrophic if one of these branches were to fall on us. We can't afford any injuries", said Victor.

The periodic gusts were so strong in the clearing ahead that the boys feared their tents would not stand up against the forces of such a formidable wind shearing across them. They had no idea what to do next.

Victor spotted a stream nearby with a steep ravine. "Let's go down there," he suggested.

Everyone jumped down into the water to escape the headwind. The steep walls on both sides of the stream, carved by many centuries of water erosion, offered some protection from violent turbulence above. Unfortunately, they were standing in about a foot of water.

Dion momentarily thought, then instructed the others, "Each of you go find a couple of branches about eight feet in length and three inches in diameter."

No one knew what he had planned, but he gave the orders with such authority that he clearly had an idea worth considering. The others climbed out of the steep creek bed and looked around for the right-sized branches. They were not hard to find. The wind had broken so many considerable-sized branches out of the nearby trees. They each dragged several of them to the edge of the stream, fighting the wind with every step.

Then Dion said, "I think we can use our tent to make a hammock across two branches. The integrated tent ropes, the ones that are normally used for securing the tent to the ground, can be used to attach our tents to the branches."

Nate was still unsure what they would do with hammocks once they had them made.

"Dion, what are we doing here?" he asked.

"My idea is to lay the hammocks across the stream and wedge the branches into the bank on both sides so that the hammocks are above the water level but well below the top of the ravine," he explained. "This way, we can wrap up in our sleeping bags and sleep on top of our tents. We'll be above the stream and below the ensuing wind."

It all sounded outrageous to the rest of the boys. Still, they had to admit that it felt very comfortable once they were settled into their hammocks over the stream.

As Nate snuggled in, he realized that they might not have found fresh water if they had not chosen this path earlier in the day. They may not have encountered this stream in a steep ravine protecting them from the harsh wind. It occurred to him that many decisions are like that.

If you make the right choice, things go well, but if you make one wrong turn, you can spend a tremendous amount of energy just trying to get back to where you were, he thought. *Yet, when faced with a decision with little knowledge, you must take your best guess and move on.*

The trick, he realized, was to identify a mistake as soon as possible. He decided to call this his 'fail fast and move on' strategy. *Who knows, perhaps I can use this someday.*

* * *

About that time, Brandon was reaching the summit of Majestic Mountain from the far side. He pushed forward as hard as he could all day to reach the top of the mountain by nightfall. There was far less wind on that side, so he made good progress. For the first time during this trip, he was genuinely concerned. He gave Phillip a call. Phillip was just at the base of the mountain leading into Sharefield, where the expedition had started.

"I am going to head into town to inform everyone of the situation," Phillip told Brandon. "The boys have been out on that mountain for two days and a night. We have not been in touch with them since yesterday morning. I am concerned but not panicking. We trained them well before the trip. I feel like they were prepared and are probably okay."

However, he knew that the townspeople, particularly the boy's parents, would react much differently. It was time to get them involved, regardless of the consequences.

Because of the severe wind at the top of Majestic Mountain, Brandon knew he could not light a fire. He found a small cave to shelter himself from the ferocious gust at the summit. He had agreed with Phillip to sleep there, then to return down the other side of the mountain in the morning, hoping to run into the boys on their way up. Brandon reasoned that they must have somehow stayed on the original trail since he saw no signs of them all day on the alternate path.

As Phillip walked into town, he ran directly into Anthony's father, who was surprised to see him. Phillip told Anthony's dad what had happened over the past two days. Before he could finish, Anthony's dad was running down the street yelling for help—a reaction Phillip had anticipated.

Within an hour, the townspeople had assembled and were planning a rescue effort. It was just turning dark by this time. It would be risky and probably fruitless to begin the search that evening. The plan was for the townspeople to surround the entire base of the mountain first thing in the morning and then climb up in unison until the boys were found.

In all the haste, neither Lucia nor Kim was made aware of the situation. Their parents were not part of the rescue effort. It turned out that the boys' parents, who were frantically busy preparing for the morning search effort, had completely forgotten that the girls had been tracking their friends with the GPS app.

9

MAJESTIC MOUNTAIN: DAY THREE

The sun rose quickly as the townspeople had spent many hours late into the evening pulling together last-minute supplies for the search. They thought that, as a large group, they would surely find the boys in a day, even if they had to make their way up to the mountain's summit.

* * *

The boys woke up early in their cots, too. By morning, these makeshift hammocks did not seem as comfortable as they had the night before, and now that they were somewhat rested, they couldn't wait to get out of them. The gang packed their sleeping bags and untied their tents from the branches used to make their beds.

Anthony said that he had slept well on his 'cozy cot.' Besides getting their feet wet when they stepped into the stream, the hammocks served them well under the extreme circumstances.

It was first thing in the morning when Nate started talking about his *'fail fast and move on'* thoughts from the night before.

"Okay, philosopher," said Dion. "Get your backpack ready to go."

Nate grimaced, "I understand. I'll explain it another day."

Dion kindly smiled at him as he disassembled his cot and put his tent back into his backpack.

The others were not in the mood for this type of discussion. Nate realized that the timing of sharing these sorts of insights was important.

They need to be offered when others are receptive so they will not be rejected altogether. This is not the time. After all, we are headed for the peak of Majestic Mountain, he thought.

Fortunately, the wind had quieted down overnight.

"It looks like smooth sailing up to the summit this morning," Victor scrunched his nose as he looked up.

They could see it off in the distance and judged it to be about two hours away. After a quick breakfast of instant oats made from the water they had boiled the day before and some dried fruit, they started on their way.

* * *

According to plan, Brandon got up early, packed his gear, and headed out of the sheltered cave. He started down the main trail on the opposite side of the mountain he had come up the day before. He was confident he would find the boys soon.

The trail that deceptively appeared to go straight up to the summit the boys had taken the afternoon before, and the main trail that Brandon was currently descending on were only a couple hundred yards apart in certain spots. He somehow felt he was close to the boys. Although out of sight, they passed each other on separate trails.

Around mid-morning, the gang finally reached the top of Majestic Mountain. They cheered and celebrated with homemade brownies, mixed in with a bit of horseplay, born out of sheer jubilation of their accomplishment.

They knew the trip down the back side of the mountain would be much easier since it was a gentle incline. In terms of distance, it was a little longer than the uphill climb but much easier to navigate. Everyone felt confident they would accomplish their goal and finish this fantastic expedition.

As the boys sat at the summit, looking out over the vast farmland below, it was as if they could see forever. Just then, Victor looked down at the ground and saw something so strange he could hardly believe his own eyes. It was a rock, but not just any rock. This one looked almost identical to the one in their school play, under which the magic key was found.

In an excited voice, Victor said, "Look, everyone, this is the rock from our play!"

As Dion gazed at the rock, his mind shifted from the present to what was bothering him before this mountain expedition. He was still waiting to tell the gang about the key he found under the waterfalls at the base of Majestic Mountain. Now the rock in their theater production appeared here on top of the mountain. *How could this possibly be a coincidence?* he thought.

Everyone was wondering what could be under that mysterious rock.

Nate gasped, "This is unbelievable."

Victor's curiosity got the best of him. He grabbed hold of the far side of the rock with both hands, then, with a quick jerk, he pulled the rock toward him. The forceful pull caused it to roll over at his feet. To everyone's surprise, there was something under the rock, but it was nothing they would have expected. It was a caterpillar. A caterpillar of the monarch butterfly species, easily recognizable by its bright yellow coloring with black stripes.

"Wow!" Victor exclaimed as he picked up the larva on a stick, then put it into the mason jar he had brought with the peaches inside.

Anthony had read about the mystical monarch butterfly in school. He said, "Do you know that the last generation monarch butterflies of the summer migrate thousands of miles to warmer climates where they spend the winter, only to return to where they left the following summer? The strange thing about this migration is that the returning butterflies are not the same ones that left the year before. They are offspring that somehow know how to navigate back to where the previous generations had left!"

He said the larva in the jar would transform into a chrysalis and emerge as a beautiful butterfly within about two weeks.

Nate asked, "How could nature have figured all this out? Simply amazing!"

As amazing as everything was on the boys' end, things weren't as fun down the mountain.

* * *

As they had planned, the search party of townspeople, including Phillip and the boys' dads, surrounded the mountain at sunup and began walking upward toward the summit from all directions. Their progress was slow because they checked every side path, gully, and thick bush for any sign of the boys.

Kim and Lucia had previously signed up for a short one-day volleyball summer camp that started that morning. By then, they had heard about the situation and were aware of the search party on their way to find the gang. They were both distraught with worry.

Kim made it her highest priority to call Dion's father at the base of the mountain and tell him that she and Lucia could chart their friends' progress for the first day up to Camp Y Knot and beyond, but they lost signal after that.

The search party passed the waterfall to the Wandering River bridge by early afternoon. The water had subsided, so the bridge was passable. The rescue team had found nothing of interest until that time. Then, under a tree, a local barber happened upon the torn shirt that Victor had left behind after crossing the lake that had formed downstream of the flooded bridge.

Of course, this generated considerable panic among the boys' families and led to a quick change in the search strategy.

Most of the search party congregated at the Wandering River Bridge. They began following the river downstream toward the waterfall, looking for any signs of the boys. Some of the rescue party advanced toward Camp Y Knot in response to the phone call from Kim to Dion's father, but there was nothing they could find that'd tell them their sons were safe and sound.

Yet another group of searchers continued up the mountain at various locations around its perimeter. Forward progress was even slower because this rescue team was tasked with examining even more territory and needed to be thorough so that they would not miss anything.

* * *

Oblivious to the panic among their neighbors, friends, and families, the gang of friends was preparing to head down the back side of the mountain.

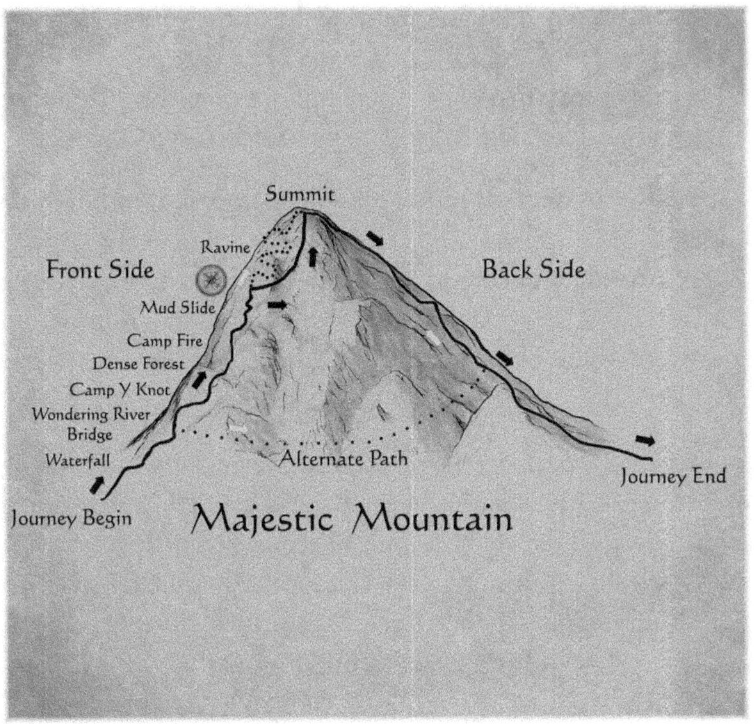

At the same time, Brandon was following the main trail the boys had traveled up over the previous two days. The boys had not made a fire on their way up the main trail since the first night of their adventure, which barely showed there had been any human activity.

So naturally, Brandon did not see evidence of them as he hiked down that path. He was quite an outdoorsy man but not an expert tracker who might have been able to recognize signs that the boys had recently been there.

* * *

After thoroughly enjoying the view from the top of Majestic Mountain, the boys started their journey home. They were eager to share all their experiences but not in *too* big of a hurry. They had no idea that half the town was looking for them!

Their third day was rather leisurely compared to the previous two. They walked along the trail, stopping every hour or so for a drink. Lunch was the same food they had eaten the past few days. They were running low on rations but figured they would be at the bottom of the mountain sometime early the following morning.

The crew coming toward them from below was checking everything in their path. As the day progressed, the multiple rescue teams were all becoming discouraged. The boys were taking their time coming down, stopping frequently to enjoy the scenery and recount their adventures upward on the challenging side of Majestic Mountain.

The gang was casually walking along when Anthony suddenly stopped. He spotted a sprawling, intricate spiderweb directly in front of him. It was fully visible in all its glory from the shadowed light beaming down between several tall trees. The web was constructed into four equal quadrants. Everyone marveled at its meticulous detail after he pointed it out.

"Look at its complexity and precision," Anthony commented. "That is a Masterpiece Stringy Quartet if I have ever seen one."

Nate laughed. "Only you would say something like that."

Victor remarked, "I learned in science class that spider web thread is stronger than steel of the same thickness."

Just then, Anthony spotted a massive black hairy spider, bigger than any he had ever seen. "There is our spider, Zippy Line."

As Zippy Line moved toward the boys, Anthony said, "Maybe it is time for us to move along before we become hopelessly *entangled*."

They weren't too keen on seeing what kind it was since it could be venomous.

They laughed at the joke as they walked down the trail; everyone was in a good mood. On one of their stops, Anthony, still wearing that silly 'Tupper Tough' baseball hat he had made the day before, started hitting small rocks from a stream with a branch that he used as a baseball bat.

Nate was happy to be heading home but was puzzled by the rock he had seen atop the mountain.

Dion was equally puzzled and asked, "What do you suppose that rock was doing up there on top of the mountain?"

Nate shook his head. "I don't know. I guess it was doing what rocks usually do, just lying around."

"Very funny, you know what I mean."

"Yes, but I have no idea why there was a rock at the top of Majestic Mountain like in our play. Pretty strange, I would say."

Dion agreed.

* * *

About an hour before dark, Brandon was reaching the site where the boys had made a fire on the first evening of their trip. He immediately called the search crew to tell them of his discovery. Some of the searchers were still probing the area along the Wandering River, where Victor's shirt was found, while others were inspecting the area around Camp Y Knot and into the forest beyond, based on the GPS information from Kim and Lucia.

Brandon told the search party that the boys must have passed the Wandering River bridge and beyond Camp Y Knot. The search crews on that side of the mountain immediately began to hike through the dense forest toward Brandon while he continued his descent.

A few of them stayed behind to continue looking for more signs of the boys in the lower parts of the trail. In the meantime, the rescuers on the other side of the mountain continued their search from the backside, moving, ever so slowly, directly toward the boys.

The group traveling through the woods on the front side met up with Brandon about an hour later. They had seen no sign of the boys other than Victor's torn shirt and a fresh campfire site that was likely theirs. It was getting dark, and hopes were being squashed. The rescue group on the backside of the mountain decided to descend to near the bottom and wait till morning before continuing.

The plan was for the group on the front side to spend the night at Camp Y Knot. There were some cabins there they could use for lodging. The Sharefield Fire Department had lined up two helicopters from a neighboring town to scour the mountain from the air, starting first thing in the morning.

That night, none of the townspeople slept well.

Worried, Kim told Lucia, "I am determined to join the search in the morning."

Lucia agreed. "I am so scared for them. Let's just show up at the bottom of the far side of the mountain first thing in the morning and join the search crew there."

"Yeah, let's do it."

IO

MAJESTIC MOUNTAIN: DAY FOUR

While everyone back home was riddled with anxiety and paranoia, all the boys were feeling quite relaxed. They were only a few hours from the base of the mountain when they decided to stop for the day.

The search crew had retreated down to the mountain base just in front of the boys before dark. The boys thought they would be home well before noon, less than half a day later than originally planned.

They ate the last preserved food, setting aside oats and dried fruit for their typical breakfast the following morning.

They went to bed early on that warm summer night, feeling relaxed and proud that they had come this far.

The next morning, Dion was the first one up. The sun was just rising in the east, as he yawned and enthusiastically woke everyone, saying, "Let's finish our journey and head for home!"

At about the same time, the two helicopters took off from town to search for the boys. The townspeople, including Kim and Lucia, were at the base of the mountain, ready to resume their search. Phillip and Brandon had spent the previous evening on the phone, retracing every step and wondering how they could have missed the boys and why they had lost contact with them.

The helicopter on the downward side of the mountain had not been in the air for more than twenty minutes before it spotted the gang walking along the open trail through a prairie. The co-pilot immediately called the leader of the search team on the radio and told him that all four boys had been found.

Everyone searching for the boys was extremely relieved to hear the good news. The helicopter quickly circled and dropped to an altitude just above the group. The boys had no idea what was going on. They just waved and cheered before continuing their trek down the mountain.

"It appears the helicopter is trying to land here in the prairie," Dion said.

"That is strange," remarked Nate.

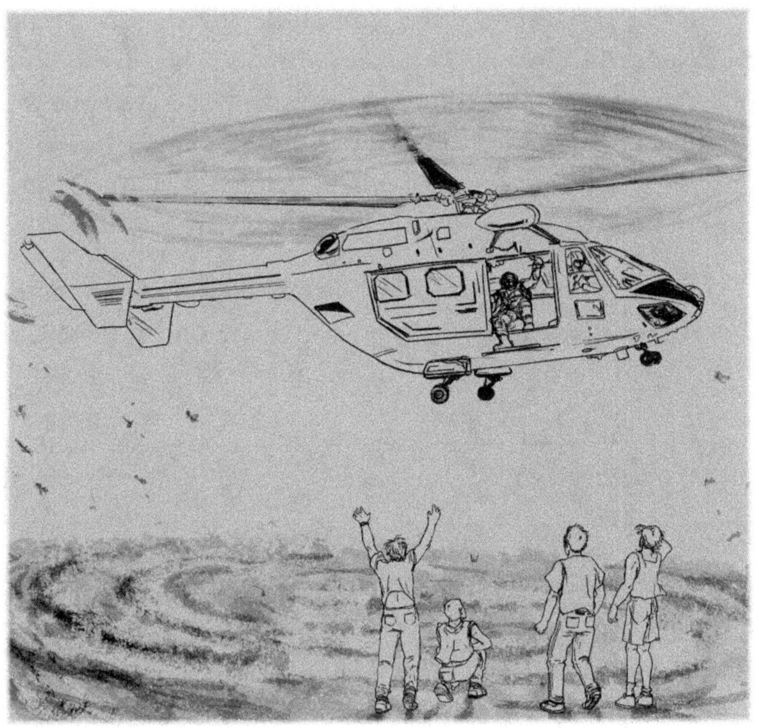

The boys stopped to watch the action.

"Now *that* is a Squirrelly Whirly," said Anthony.

Soon, the chopper was on the ground. The pilot and co-pilot emerged from the helicopter. They ran toward the boys, just standing there observing the spectacle. Their first impulse was to start running away from these strange men who were very obviously after them and had military-level gear with them. Panic-stricken Victor took off first, and everyone followed him as the pilots chased after them.

They got close enough to yell, "Wait, we are here to help you!"

So, the boys stopped, but somewhat apprehensively. The pilot quickly caught up with them with his palms in the air to show his peaceful intentions. He explained how everyone was looking for them and fearing the worst. The boys felt terrible that they had lost contact with Brandon and Phillip. They never thought of it as a life-threatening situation.

Dion told the chopper pilot, "We are doing fine and want to finish our journey on our own. We are only a couple of hours from the base of Majestic Mountain."

The pilot reluctantly agreed and returned to the chopper and radioed everyone in the search party informing them of the boys' plan.

As the boys arrived at the base of the mountain, a sizable crowd of people was waiting for them. Over half the town was there, including Lucia and Kim. Everyone was cheering, treating them like heroes coming home from combat. It was bizarre.

Sure, we'd had a few challenges along the way, but the trip was everything we had hoped it would be and more, thought Nate.

Each of the boys was happy to be home. Victor, who had planned so extensively for this journey, realized that not everything had gone exactly as he had expected, but if he and his friends had not done so much preparation before the trip, things could have turned out a lot worse.

All their parents and Kim and Lucia agreed to meet for lunch at the Mustang Pizza restaurant: they had great Italian food. It was Anthony's favorite place to eat. Whenever the gang wanted to go out, he suggested they go for 'Pepperoni at the Pony.'

"I will have a pizza with everything on it," Nate said. That pizza sure tasted good after a diet of dried foods for the past three days.

Each of the hikers shared experiences of their epic adventure with their parents. Brandon and Phillips' account of the paths they took, along with those of the boys, started to make sense to everyone — a combination of unexpected circumstances and a rather unlikely sequence of events created so much confusion.

Kim and Lucia listened intently to every word. They were so thankful that things turned out well in the end. Lucia commented, "We were justified in worrying when we lost the GPS signal after that first day."

To which Kim replied, "I am just glad we are all here together." She looked up from her plate and glanced at Dion.

As Nate sat listening to his friends' accounts of their mountain adventures, it occurred to him that this sort of confusion might happen frequently. A few wrong assumptions or a lack of communication between parties, combined with unexpected events, can lead to monumental misunderstandings.

Regardless of their terrific trip, the boys were grateful to be home. It felt especially good to them to know just how much others cared about them. After lunch, the boys went home to take much-needed showers. The hot water pounding on their backs never felt so soothing. It felt equally comforting to be home and sleep in their beds after several days of camping and makeshift beds that were either too hard or hanging in the air.

Nate slept late into the following day. By that afternoon, he and his friends were all upbeat when they met with Brandon and Phillip, who wanted to go over the trip in more detail.

Brandon started the conversation, saying, "We must figure out exactly how you boys managed to go up and down Majestic Mountain completely on your own."

Brandon and Phillip listened to the boys' recount of the mountain adventure with admiration for their resourcefulness. At the same time, they were a little upset that they did not turn around and abandon their journey immediately after their phones fell into the lake.

"Anyway," said Philip, "we are thankful to have you all back home and safe."

Dion was right when he said he did not think it would be an uneventful journey. They would remember the mountain trip for some time to come.

II

THE OLD MANSION

Soon after they got home, Dion took the key he had found at the waterfalls from its special hiding place in his room. After the trip up the mountain, he marveled at it with more intensity.

Following their meeting with Brandon and Phillip earlier that afternoon, the four boys went off by themselves to their usual meeting spot, Sharefield Park. Kim was finishing her summer league softball game—another great victory for the team. Lucia was there to cheer her on.

After the game, the girls joined, and they sat under a large shade tree.

Dion took a deep breath and finally decided to reveal his big secret, "I have something to share with you."

He slowly pulled the key out of his pocket and held it up for everyone to see. He told the story of finding it behind the waterfalls and how it flickered in the sunlight in groups of three, just like in their school play!

His friends' reaction was exactly what he had expected.

"It looks remarkably like the key in our play," Victor gasped.

Dion said, "I was waiting to share it until I could fully grasp its significance, but after the journey up the mountain and all the strange occurrences that had happened there, I knew it was time to reveal this."

They all swore to keep the key a secret until they could figure out the mystery behind it.

When Victor went home that evening, he was surprised to see that the colorful caterpillar in the jar he had carried down from the top of Majestic Mountain had disappeared.

It had transformed into a chrysalis on the stick he had placed in the jar.

The next day, he showed it around to all his friends.

"Wow!" said Anthony. "That Squirm Worm will transform and become a Flutter Fly."

They were all so amazed that they couldn't bring themselves to laugh at another of Anthony's names.

"The chrysalis is made from a layer of skin of the larva," Lucia explained.

Nate said, "Well, whatever it is, it's magical."

The Sharefield Gang continued to enjoy their summer break with frequent trips to the park and the local swimming pool despite the magical key's constant presence in their heads. The days seemed to fly by. Victor had placed the jar with the chrysalis on his kitchen windowsill to get a better view.

As if the larva had a calendar, while he watched it one morning, the chrysalis broke open, and a beautiful monarch butterfly emerged!

After breakfast that morning, Dion and Nate had just arrived at Victor's house and saw the butterfly's epic unfolding. Victor said as he unscrewed the lid to the jar, "It looks magnificent! It had the classic, bright orange-and-black markings of the species. It appears to be already fully grown. Wow, it is incredibly energetic."

After it made its way clear out of the chrysalis, it quickly fluttered from the jar and was almost out of sight. Then, suddenly, it turned around and came back toward the boys. It bounced through the gentle breeze like a gymnast on a trampoline, then landed on Dion's hand for a few seconds before it flew away. This time, never to be seen again.

Dion was shocked. "This feels like an omen of some sort. It is too unusual to be coincidental."

A week later, as Nate's dad was reading the news at breakfast, he mumbled something.

Nate asked, "What is so interesting?"

His dad said, "The old man who lived in the big mansion at the edge of town has just passed away."

Dion knew no one ever saw him around. It appeared from the outside as though no one lived there at all.

Nate's dad continued, "His house will go up for auction very soon."

When Nate was younger, he thought the house was haunted and stayed away. So did his friends. There were stories around town that strange things happened up there.

The auction was to take place the following Saturday morning.

Nate told his friend Victor, "Why don't we show up at the event just for fun? It would be interesting to see who might purchase a property that looked like it hasn't been lived in for decades, even though the lonely old man just recently died."

The two boys agreed and showed up that Saturday morning right on time. The bidding started with no lower limit. There were a few bids from the locals, but no one seemed to really want the property, except for one couple who kept over-bidding whenever anyone made an offer. Nate and Victor couldn't imagine why they would want the old place so badly.

Finally, after several rounds of back-and-forth bidding, that couple won the auction. They seemed elated.

"I can't believe someone bought that house. It looks like a mess," said Victor.

Nate agreed. "From what we can see on the outside, it needs a lot of work."

When Kim found out that Nate and Victor attended the auction of the old mansion, she wanted to know if there was anyone there from around town that might have happened to mention their class theater production.

She asked Nate, "Did you hear anything at all that would shed some light on who the mystery author of our school play might be?"

Nate replied, "Not really. I overheard the lady that bought the place say to her husband during the bidding that she was on edge and hoped that they got the keys to the place. I thought her wording was a little funny at the time, but it was probably just coincidence."

After hearing the talk around town, it became clear why this couple wanted to purchase the property so badly. The old man was related to them on the wife's side of the family.

Nate told Victor, "According to what I hear, they plan to fix the place up and use it as a bed-and-breakfast."

Victor responded, "That's pretty cool. There's not a lot of lodging in Sharefield."

"Yeah," said Nate, "as you know, during the summer, the baseball tournaments attract visitors from out of town. Often, they have to stay in neighboring towns because of Sharefield's scarcity of hotels. Our family often lets guests stay with us in our home for a weekend event."

"I remember," said Victor. "Having someone new around is always a lot of fun for you and the rest of us."

The new owners were thinking about renovating the old mansion right away. They wanted it to reflect the town and its people. Kim saw a sign on a telephone pole asking for help to clean the place up inside, along with the grounds. She told the rest of the Sharefield Gang about the opportunity.

"If we take on this part-time job together, we can complete it in a week. We can make some extra money, not to mention that we will see the inside of that place. We can find out if it is haunted or not."

That did sound very appealing to the rest of the gang.

"I am all in favor of doing this," said Lucia.

Anthony wasn't so sure. He stood up and began walking like a zombie. Everyone knew that he was only joking, but there was a hint of fear in his crazy antics.

Dion tried to convince his friend, "Look, it will be another new chapter in our summer of adventure."

Victor shrugged. "Okay, I am ready to take on the haunted house and whatever uncertainties it brings."

"So," said Nate, "we are all in. Sign us up!"

The couple who bought the house were delighted to have the help. They told the gang they would need to wait a couple of weeks before starting the work because some necessary business had to be taken care of before renovation of the property could begin. The gang waited anxiously for the start date, wondering what was inside this dilapidated old mansion on the hill.

Finally, the week to clean up the soon-to-be Victorian bed and breakfast had arrived. The Sharefield Gang met in the park early that Monday morning before walking together to the edge of town to begin their assignment. The couple who bought the place met the gang at the door and invited them in. The mansion looked haunted. Dust was all over the old furnishings, and the place smelled musty. Spiderwebs lined the doorways between the parlor, living room, and kitchen.

The couple introduced themselves, "Hello, I am Daniel Martinez, and this is my wife, Claire Martinez. Who do we have here?"

The gang proceeded to say their names one at a time. The couple beamed at all of them as they introduced themselves.

Kim thought, *Well, they seem really nice.*

Daniel told the gang, "The old man who previously owned this house never used these rooms downstairs. He was not well and stayed mostly in his upstairs bedroom."

After a quick tour of the grounds, the friends decided they would work downstairs on the first day, move outside to do the work in the yard on Tuesday and Wednesday, then return to clean the living quarters upstairs on Thursday and then finish everything up by the end of the week.

Monday was a lot of fun as the gang cleaned and dusted off the old furniture and the ornate woodwork that adorned the fireplace, baseboards, and crown molding. While they worked, they made it a game to see who could come up with the scariest story about the mansion's past and who might have visited there in days gone by. Through their imagination, everyone from Abraham Lincoln to Susan B. Anthony graced the halls of this old Victorian mansion.

The time flew by quickly. By the end of the day, everyone was tired but upbeat as they went home for dinner.

"This was more fun than I expected," said Lucia. "I like this place. It has a character all its own."

The others were equally satisfied. When Nate got up Tuesday morning, he looked forward to spending the day at the mansion. All day, the gang went up and down the hill to the mansion, working on the grounds.

They pulled weeds, trimmed bushes, painted fences, and so much more. A long hedge on the side of the property needed trimming.

Lucia suggested, "Maybe we can tie a tensioned string from end-to-end of the hedge so that we can cut it straight and even."

After finishing that job, Dion remarked, "Lucia, your string idea worked out perfectly."

"Landscaping is hard work," sighed Victor.

They were all dirty and tired by the end of the second day. They met that evening after dinner at the local ice cream stand for dessert and to hang out and enjoy the warm summer evening. Dion brought up the key again, asking his friends if they had any new insights about its purpose.

"A key of great value should open a treasure chest, right?" offered Anthony.

Nate said, "Doubt we will find one of those in Sharefield."

Then Kim opened her purse and pulled out the locket she had shown to Lucia while the boys were on the mountain.

Dion noticed it right away.

"Let me see the picture inside," he said. Kim handed it to him. He quickly, almost nervously, opened it up. "Wow, that's a very nice picture of you. Where did you get this locket?"

"I purchased it with my own money that I earned doing work around our house."

"I really like it."

I had it printed off of a selfie on my phone. I will send it to you." With that she grabbed her phone and forwarded the picture to Dion, while asking, "Do you have any good pictures of yourself?"

Dion looked at her picture on his phone and smiled to himself, then sent off one of himself over to her.

The two of them were smiling as the gang headed for home before dark.

On Wednesday, they finished the work outside. Thursday, they were back inside the mansion, tasked with cleaning the upstairs, where the old man had spent most of his time. It was not as dusty up there, but there was still plenty to do to get everything in order so the new owners could have a paying guest stay in any of its seven bedrooms.

As Anthony dusted the long hallway, he noticed a square break in the plaster along one wall. Kim and Dion were working in the next room when Anthony called them to the hallway.

Kim looked at the square line in the broken plaster and said, "Maybe it's a door."

Dion said, "I don't think so. It is not the height of a door, less than four feet square, but it does look like it should move. Why don't we give it a push?"

Kim pushed on one edge while Dion went on the other. The wall swung inward on Kim's side, revealing a winding flight of stairs leading to the mansion's attic.

"Whoa!"

When it was time for their afternoon break, they all gathered in the hallway and decided to climb the steps to the attic. At the time, Mr. and Mrs. Martinez worked in the small utility building adjacent to the house.

The stairway was only wide enough for one person. Kim said, "I will go first." She ducked her head under the low doorway and started up the stairs. After climbing only a few steps, she was met with torrid air from the stuffy air in the enclosed space above. She gasped, saying in desperation, "The air up here is so hot that I can hardly breathe. We will not be able to stay here long." Dion, who was following right behind her, remarked, "That is for sure." The rest of the gang slowly made their way up the winding steps, feeling the oppressive heat with every step.

Fortunately, they were greeted with suitable, solid flooring underfoot below the angled ceiling that formed the mansion's roof from the outside. As they reached the top of the stairs, they all began to sweat.

"This heat is unbearable," Dion groaned.

Anthony replied, "Don't you talk about bears again like the last time!"

A pull string at the top of the steps turned on one dull lightbulb near where they were standing. As Nate looked around, he saw some beautiful old wood molding that must have been removed from some of the rooms and stored up there. There was a decorative old chest with several hand-crocheted afghans and several stacks of papers.

Victor said, "Nothing looks all that interesting."

They were just about to head back downstairs when Dion spotted an old, square leather briefcase that resembled a miniature suitcase. He tried to open it, but it was locked.

He sat it back on the floor next to a stack of old magazines and books, then headed for the stairs to escape the sweltering heat. Anthony and Victor followed close behind him.

Nate was just in front of Kim. Walking toward the stairs, she noticed a loose stack of papers held together with a binder clip. She picked it up. Much to her surprise, the cover sheet read *The Script*. She flipped to the second page but could not distinguish the small print in the dim light.

As Nate started down the steps, Kim brought the papers toward the stairway light, where she could see well enough to read.

Suddenly, she realized this was the manuscript of the school play they had just performed before summer began. Kim quickly flipped to the back and saw a new section called *Missing Information and Continuation of the Mystery.*

Dion, Anthony, and Victor were already back downstairs in the hallway. Nate was on the steps.

Kim called to him, "Nate, come back up here!"

She was astounded, "Arthur Herring, our bus driver, signed the last page of the manuscript."

Nate saw it for himself, saying, "This is unbelievable."

By then, they were both dripping with sweat from the oppressive heat. Kim set the manuscript on the floor next to the stairway, and the two of them quickly headed down the stairs to join the others. Once in the hallway, they could hardly imagine what they had just found.

Nate told the others, "Believe it or not, Kim found a copy of *The Script* up there. We saw it for real!"

Anthony thought it must be some joke. "Yeah, and there was a treasure chest up there too."

The look on Kim's face showed that she was no-nonsense and serious. "It is up there."

Dion said, "That is almost too amazing to be true."

But it was.

* * *

That evening, the Sharefield Gang met in the park after dinner. All they could talk about was the manuscript that Kim had found. They could hardly believe that the playwright was their bus driver, Arthur. Did he write the play?

Lucia and Kim told the boys the story of their visit to the outdoor supply store while the boys were on the mountain.

Anthony replied, "I guess Arthur would not be considered an ideal outdoorsman in need of a compass."

To which Victor said, "Maybe not, but I can certainly think of others that the old man at the store might think of as less likely."

The gang asked so many questions among themselves with no answers in mind. How did the manuscript end up in the attic of the old mansion? What part of the story was missing, and what happened after the key was found?

The next morning, the gang returned to the mansion for their last work day. They could not believe how quickly the week had gone by. Claire instructed them to go through the house one last time to make sure that everything was clean and in order.

Daniel said that all the trash should be left in the hallways. A trash collection service would come the following morning to pick up anything in the hallways, attic, or utility building and take it to the city dump. Dion looked at Kim; the rest of the gang knew what they were thinking.

After finishing their work downstairs, the gang quickly moved to the upstairs bedrooms. They had done a thorough job the day before, so there was not a lot of work remaining. When they had a chance, Nate opened the rotating square door at the end of the hallway, and everyone headed up the steps to the attic.

It was a cooler day; they would be more comfortable up there and not sweaty like the day before. When Dion reached the top, he pulled the cord to turn on the light. He did not see the manuscript next to the stairway. Kim was the last one to leave the attic the day before and pointed to the exact place on the floor where she had left it.

Everyone started rummaging around the attic, frantically looking for the manuscript, but it was nowhere to be found.

"What could have happened to it…" Kim wondered.

That's what everyone wanted to know.

Just when they were about to lose hope, Dion spotted the square leather briefcase he had seen the day before. On a hunch and remembering the comments that had been made about opening a treasure chest, he had put his 'keep' in his pocket that morning.

He took out the key and tried to insert it into the keyhole of the briefcase. The gang all stood around him and watched. They were wondrously amazed as the key rotated in the slot!

Dion exclaimed, "It unlocked!"

He slowly opened the lid of the mysterious briefcase. Everyone's eyes grew large as they peered inside. To their disbelief, they saw what looked to be an old, retro portable computer. It had a keyboard built right into the top of a big, boxy-looking white machine.

Dion pulled it out of the briefcase. "The nameplate reads *Commodore 64*."

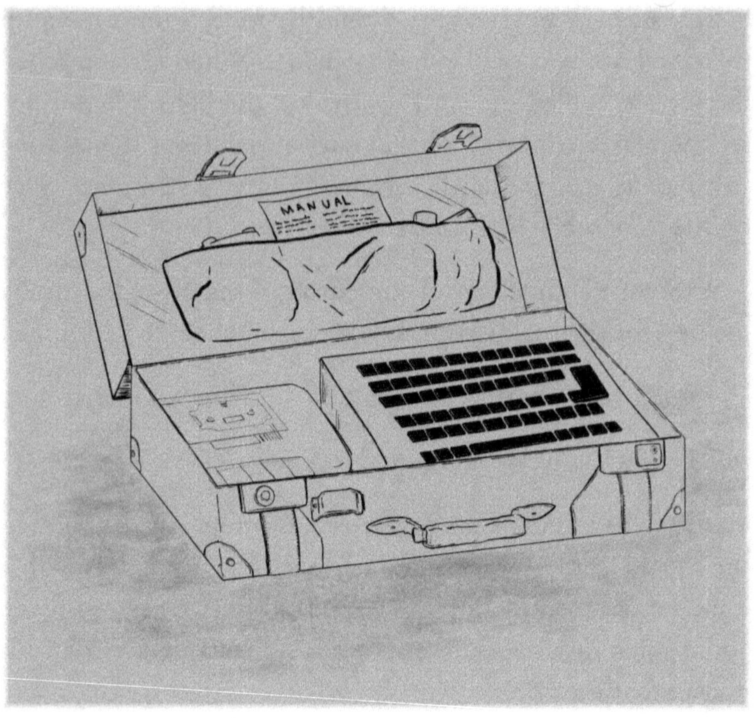

It was no manuscript, but they could look for answers there at least.

"What a strange find," said Lucia.

There was another box beside the computer that looked like an old cassette player. It also said 'Commodore' on it.

"Take a look inside the flap in the lid," Victor instructed.

There, Dion found a power cord, manuals, and assorted cables.

Kim knew a little bit about the history of computers because her dad was an early home computer owner and talked about them frequently. She explained to the group that old-time computers did not have a display.

"They required a separate monitor to see the graphic output. Data was stored on big five-and-a-quarter-inch floppy disks requiring a special disk reader or Datasette that looks like old cassette tapes."

Dion realized the other piece next to the computer must be a Datasette player. He opened the lid and said, "Look, there is indeed a Datasette inside!"

Just then, Victor, standing guard by the steps to the attic, heard a call from below.

It was Mr. Martinez saying, "It is time to close up the house for the day."

Knowing that the waste disposal service was coming to take everything out of the house the following morning, the group decided to save it and take the old computer home.

Dion took the main unit, which filled his backpack. Nate took the Datasette player and put it in his. Kim grabbed the manuals, power cord, and cables and put them in her backpack.

Off they went toward the steps from the attic. They made one last search for the missing manuscript, but it was nowhere to be found. This was a real disappointment because that manuscript could answer so many of their questions.

Was their bus driver, Arthur, really the playwright? What was in the extra sections of *The Script* that were not part of their school play last year? How did the manuscript get into the attic of the mansion in the first place?

On the positive side, the gang had possession of the old computer. Maybe it'd help.

Downstairs, the couple thanked the kids for all their efforts and paid each of them well for a hard week's work.

As they were leaving, Daniel said, "If you would like, you can look in the utility shed on your way out to see if there is anything inside that you might want to keep before the waste collectors arrive in the morning to clean it out."

The gang found several old tools and medical equipment in the shed, including a wheelchair, but nothing of particular interest to them. Mr. Martinez had told them that the old man who used to live in the mansion sometimes used a wheelchair.

12

THE GAME

The friends agreed to meet at Dion's house the next day to check out the old *Commodore 64* computer. On Saturday morning, everyone arrived sometime around ten.

The evening before, Kim had done some research on the internet to learn more about the *Commodore 64*. She found out that sometimes a TV with a component video input jack would work to display the video content.

Dion's family had an older TV in the basement with this input port. The extra cables that Kim brought from the attic with the computer fit snugly into the back of the TV.

As everyone watched, Dion plugged the computer into the wall outlet, connected the cassette to the computer, and turned it on. It seemed to take forever for anything to happen, although it was only a minute or so. Then, some green text appeared on the screen, along with a flashing arrow.

The date on the screen said January 9, 1988.

"That was the last time this computer was used!" voiced Nate.

Everyone was astounded that it still worked after all this time. Kim had the manual in her hands and instructed Dion to access the Datasette in the external player. As soon as he did, it started to spin. After rewinding to the beginning, it reversed direction and showed a low-resolution graphic on the TV screen.

It was the title of a game called *Scavenger Hunt*.

The clueless gang looked to Kim for some clarity.

"Many games were written for the *Commodore 64* by early programmers," she explained. "These programs were typically simple adventure games that involved finding different objects to solve a puzzle. In fact, the *Commodore 64* remains the most popular computer of all time to this day. Thousands of such games have been written for it."

The computer only displayed sixteen colors. The output images were very low-resolution and pixelated. Still, one could see what was being shown on the screen and move around the chunky-looking display with the mouse.

Everyone was thrilled that the old computer still worked and wanted to play *Scavenger Hunt*. Dion jumped in and started the game, bringing up a screen of text describing the background for the scavenger hunt.

A small midwest town wants to raise money for their local hospital. Gift certificates were solicited from each of the businesses in town and locked in a treasure chest on display in front of city hall. The townspeople have all donated money to participate in the hunt. Players must go from business to business and gather the clues that lead to the key that will unlock the chest. The winner is entitled to a spending spree using all the gift certificates inside.

"That sounds like fun!" chirped Victor.

Dion hit the 'Next' button, and the Datasette began to spin. After a couple of minutes, it stopped. A view of the town was visible on the screen. One could see various businesses lining the main street, but the details of each could not be discerned.

Several old cars from the 1980s were parked along the street as well. Dion selected a building in the middle of the street with his mouse. The Datasette began to spin again, and a picture of a general store popped up. Dion clicked on the door, and soon, there was a picture of the inside of the store. There appeared to be nothing of interest inside, so Dion moved the game back into the street.

Next, Dion selected a building down at the edge of town. The new image that eventually appeared was the old hospital itself, up on top of a hill, with a sign in the front saying, 'Thank you for your donations.'

There appeared to be a building beside the hospital, so Dion selected the edge of the screen. To everyone's amazement, a picture popped up of an old mansion that looked strikingly like the one where the computer was found.

They all gasped!

"Could the video game have been written about Sharefield?" asked Victor.

Nate was doubtful. "That does not seem likely because the main street does not look like our town, even many years ago."

Dion clicked on everything he could, on and around the old mansion, but nothing changed.

Kim explained, "In these old games, if there were something of interest, it would bring up a new picture of the item or place once it was identified with a mouse click."

Eventually, Dion returned to the image of the main street.

Victor said, "So far, this game has not exposed any clues to solve the puzzle, but it has shown us an interesting picture that looks remarkably like the old mansion we were just cleaning this past week."

"This is very strange, indeed," agreed Lucia.

"A computer from the 1980s that knows its whereabouts today. Maybe it is having an identity crisis," said Anthony.

This time, Dion clicked on another building on the opposite side of the street. It turned out to be a sporting goods store. Dion moved inside to find the shelves stocked with activewear and equipment for every sport imaginable.

He moved toward the back of the store, and then suddenly, the Datasette began to reel. A picture of an open trapdoor appeared, which disappeared and was replaced with a picture of a basement room.

"We have clearly fallen through the trapdoor and are now in the lower storage room," Kim observed.

"Look, there's a baseball bat." Dion clicked on it.

The bat looked normal to Kim, but Victor got all excited.

"Look at the wood grain in the bat!" he said. "It looks like the image we saw of a bicycle on the Tree of Knowledge at Camp Y Knot on Majestic Mountain!"

The graphics were crude, but he was correct. Nate saw it, too. He said, "If I stare at the bat just right, I can also see the outline of a bicycle."

Now, the gang was really feeling uneasy. Nate's hands began to sweat. He said, "First, we see an image of the old mansion and now *this*. Something very strange is going on here."

There were steps leading upward, so Dion clicked on them, which took the gang back up to the store's main level and then back out onto the main street. Next, Dion selected a building that turned out to be a bakery. They went inside and were instructed to choose one of five different types of pie.

"We should select the peach pie," Victor suggested. He remembered that the bicycle he saw in the woodgrain of the Tree of Knowledge eventually led him to open the jar of peaches he had taken on their mountain journey.

Dion selected the peach pie.

Inside was a note that said, 'Go to the utility shed.'

They had picked the right pie because it was the only one with a clue inside. But all of this was becoming just too much of a coincidence. Dion left the bakery and entered the main street again.

"What utility shed?" asked Lucia. "There is no shed on the street."

Dion clicked farther up the street, which brought up an image of a 1987 Mustang. Next to the vehicle was something even stranger. It appeared to be an electric car charging station.

They all jumped out of their seats at the same time. This computer had been locked in a briefcase since 1988!

"Wait a minute, how could there be a car charging station in this game?" asked Dion.

"Yes, not to mention all of the other similarities to our recent experiences," whispered Victor.

This was creepy!

As they all thought about it, it remained quite a mystery, but at least it did make the meaning of the clue in the peach pie clear to them.

"The storage shed might be next to the image of the old mansion next to the hospital," Nate suggested. "We should go back to the mansion and see if a storage shed is nearby."

Everyone agreed that it was worth investigating. So, Dion again took the gang to the hospital on the hill and then to the mansion beside it. When he clicked on the far edge of the screen opposite the side of the hospital, sure enough, the Datasette started to spin.

A moment later, there was a picture of a utility shed. It looked very similar to the one they had just walked through the day before!

Victor didn't want to continue the game. "This is just a little bit too disturbing."

But Kim disagreed. "We have to keep going to figure all of this out."

Inside the shed was a piece of medical equipment similar to the one they had just seen yesterday. Dion clicked on the machine. An image of the equipment manufacturing plate showed up. It read 'The Medical Manufacturing Depot.'

They left the shed and returned to the main street, now looking for the Medical Manufacturing Depot. After checking out a couple of other buildings, they found it next to the sporting goods store where the baseball bat had been found.

Inside the medical building, they could see an image of wheelchairs being manufactured and some markings on the factory wall. Dion clicked on it, and it was a flying goose, a part of the company's trademark, which read *'Freedom to Fly with a Medical Wheelchair.'*

After seeing the trademark, Dion moved back out to the main street. The Datasette started spinning, bringing a new image onto the screen. It was a flock of geese overhead in 'V' formation, just like they had seen on Majestic Mountain when trying to decide which path to take.

This time, the geese pointed straight at the old bank across the street. Dion clicked on the bank, and an image of the inside of their own Sharefield Savings and Loan appeared.

The kids kept quiet as they stared at the screen before them.

Inside the bank, there were three safety deposit boxes. At the bottom of the screen was text that read, *'Choose the right box to claim the key and win the game. Choose the wrong box, and you will lose.'*

They all gazed at the three boxes. Everyone had an opinion as to which one to choose. Then Kim saw that there were tiny numbers under each box. They were low resolution and hard to make out. One of them appeared to be 845 . . . or maybe it was 896. The other two boxes started with numbers 1 and 7, respectively.

Kim said, "At the end of our school play, the key was stored in a safe deposit, box 395. Maybe what looks like an eight is actually a three, and the four may be a nine, making the number of that box 395, just like in our school play. I vote for selecting that box because the others are numbers none of us recognize."

It was a long shot, but no one had a better reason for selecting a different box. So, after a bit of discussion, they decided to go with box 395, or whatever number it was.

Dion clicked on it, and the Datasette began to spin. Either the screen would come up and say they had lost the game, or they would find the key!

After what seemed like several minutes, the Datasette stopped. The screen was filled with confetti. Then the Datasette spun again, and a picture of a key appeared! It was not just any key. It was not a key as one might expect. It was a replica of the one in the school play. The same-shaped key Dion had found behind the waterfalls that opened the briefcase containing the old computer. It was also the same key that would open the treasure chest in this game and reveal all the donated gift certificates from around town.

The Sharefield Gang was excited to have won the game and wanted to go to city hall to open the treasure chest, but they were also very puzzled by all these strange coincidences on this magical old computer.

Dion clicked the mouse and moved them back to the main street and then to city hall, where the treasure chest was located. He clicked on it, and after the Datasette did its thing, the chest opened and exposed multiple gift certificates of various amounts from all the shops in town, just as promised.

On top of the pile was a certificate from the local bookstore. Dion clicked on it, and it took them to the entrance of that store. So, as he had done several times before, Dion clicked on the entrance to the store.

After a minute or so, everyone was looking at a view of the inside of the bookstore. In the front, there was a book on display. Dion selected the generic-looking book. After another whirl of the Datasette, they could see its cover.

The book was called '*Continuation of The Script, Expanded Version.*'

They all looked at each other in shock. When they looked back at the screen, it was blank. The computer had somehow locked up. Everyone got goosebumps and a spooky feeling inside. They tried everything they could for the next hour to get the old computer to restart. But nothing worked. It appeared to be completely disabled.

By this time, it was late, so they decided to head home. The friends thanked Dion for his expert navigation through the game and Kim for her knowledge of computer history.

Kim said to Dion, "Together we were able to figure out how to get this old computer to work, at least for a little while.

We make a good team." Dion nodded and smiled at her.

As they walked home their separate ways, they all were connected by the same thought. What had they just observed? What kind of sorcery could have created such a mystical experience?

13

THE PAPER DRIVE

The Sharefield Gang wanted to find the manuscript, and they wouldn't stop at anything to get to it. After all, Kim and Nate had held it in their hands just a few days ago. The extra sections of the story seemed even more relevant to them now.

Kim and Lucia visited Mr. and Mrs. Martinez at the old mansion to ask if they knew of *The Script*. Unfortunately, there was no answer at the door. They returned several times the following week only to be greeted with the same locked front door.

Perhaps the new owners were away preparing for their final move to Sharefield, thought Lucia.

The gang decided to have a brainstorming session at the park to see if they could devise a plan to locate the mysterious script together.

As they started the session, Victor brought up the obvious first suggestion.

"Why don't we contact Arthur to see if he actually was the playwright of the masterpiece?" Arthur was a very nice older gentleman who lived a private life.

Lucia said, "We are not even sure exactly where he lives. If he wanted to take credit for the work, he would have come forward on his own long before now."

Victor acknowledged, "Yes, that is probably true. We spent months over the last school year preparing for the production. During that entire time, all that was known about the author of *The Script* was that this person was an unidentified local from the community. If Arthur is indeed the author, it is unlikely that he would reveal himself now."

Kim said, "We should still address the issue with him when we return to school. Our first day is only a few weeks away. If you guys don't want to, I can talk to him."

In the meantime, everyone wanted to do what they could to find the document Kim and Nate had seen in the attic just a week before.

"Kim and I can continue to visit the mansion in hopes of getting information about the manuscript from Mr. and Mrs.

Martinez," Lucia offered. "They are very nice. I am certain that they will help us out if they can."

"How can we get our hands on as many printed documents as possible in hopes of finding the one that interests us most?" asked Nate.

"Well, we could have a paper drive by collecting and recycling books, magazines, newspapers, and other such documents," Victor suggested.

"This would help the town clean up excess clutter, support a cleaner environment, and allow us access to lots of printed material. Maybe *The Script* will turn up in the collection of paper."

"That is an outstanding idea!" exclaimed Nate.

"My uncle owns a large warehouse at the edge of town that we could use as a collection point."

"Now all we need to do is to get the word out to the town about the project," said Kim.

Anthony volunteered, "I will ask Phillip for help. Maybe he can build a web page for us to advertise our paper drive and keep track of our progress."

Phillip was happy to do so. He put the whole thing together and had the website running within a few days. Victor called the local TV station and asked them to announce the start of the drive, referring everyone to the website. The paper drive idea had become a reality.

Over the next two weeks, printed material of all sorts came flooding in. Lucia remarked to the others, "I had no idea how much unused paper there was lying around town." People were dropping off discarded books and magazines by the carloads. Each of the friends took turns going through the material. It was a challenge to keep up with all the donations.

Initially, the gang was just looking for *The Script*, but as the days wore on, they each became interested in one topic or another. There was so much material to choose from. By far, the old magazines became some of Nate's favorites. Between drop-offs, he would page through them, glancing at the pictures and reading articles covering everything from car repair tips to space exploration and virtual reality's future. It was enriching for him.

I see more of the world this way, he thought.

Lucia gravitated to fashion magazines. She was always thinking of ways to integrate some of the latest design trends into costumes and props for theater.

Kim liked the sports articles. She told the rest of the group stories of how some of the greatest athletes got to where they are today.

"It is interesting to find out that behind all the success of star athletes, there is often a lot of hardship and sacrifice."

Anthony loved looking at comics, particularly political cartoons. He had always appreciated the humor. He said, "Humor provides insight into the way people are thinking. Most humor, particularly political cartoons, have a deeper meaning reaching far beyond the funny aspects of the cartoon itself."

Victor was most pragmatic. He liked material that specifically gave him how-to instructions. He figured, *The more I understand how to fix things, the better off I will be. One never knows when a tidbit of information will be helpful.*

Dion, on the other hand, was intrigued by mysteries. He appreciated the interactions between people who naturally see things differently. He was one of the few people who could live with a sense of ambiguity. In fact, he thrived on it.

So, the Sharefield Gang each grew in different ways by the material that continued to flood into the warehouse. Anthony affectionately referred to the place as the 'Pulp Palace.' Every day the friends took turns receiving the material. By the end of the first week, they had collected several pallets of newspapers, magazines, and books that they prepared for recycling.

However, there was still no sign of *The Script*.

As the second week of the paper drive started, Kim tried again to contact Mr. and Mrs. Martinez at the mansion. They were nowhere to be found. It was as if they had vanished into thin air. As Lucia had suspected, they were in the process of moving from out of town and were away tying up loose ends at their previous residence.

The second and final week of the paper drive was turning out to be as busy as the first. Victor again called the local TV station and had them announce the drive during the evening news.

That was pretty cool, Nate thought.

Phillip was very busy staying on top of the growing number of donations with multiple website updates. Thanks to the combined efforts and cooperation of everyone involved, this project worked like a fine-tuned machine.

To the gang's dissatisfaction, there was still no sign of the document they sought. The gang knew from the beginning that this paper drive was a long shot, but they remained hopeful that they would find at least a clue related to *The Script*.

Nate told Lucia, "If just one clue turns up that leads us to *The Script*, this will have all been worth it."

She agreed. "Well, either way, we are helping Sharefield."

Everyone in town was participating by donating material. Brandon and Phillip pitched in and helped stack the media on additional pallets so all the paper could easily be transported for recycling.

The Thursday before the end of the drive, it rained heavily. That slowed down the continuous flow of donations and allowed the group to get caught up.

Friday turned out to be another story altogether. It was a bright, sunny day in late summer. Everyone who had waited until the last minute was bringing in their material for recycling.

At times there were several cars backed up waiting to make donations. The entire Sharefield Gang spent that last day at the warehouse, checking every document for any sign of *The Script*.

Kim sighed. "I am drained. I hope this is all worth it."

By that afternoon, the exhausted Sharefield Gang realized there was little hope of retrieving a copy of *The Script*. At five that evening, the last donations were packed, and everyone left to have dinner with their families.

Victor said, "I know we're disappointed that we could not locate *The Script*, but we have done a great service for the town."

That evening on TV, the local news anchor acknowledged their work for the community.

Everyone in the gang felt a sense of pride as they watched it, but despite that happiness, there was still a sinking feeling of defeat.

14

AN EXPLANATION

The next day, an ice cream social at the park was sponsored by the Sharefield Parks and Recreation Department.

The Sharefield Gang agreed to meet in the afternoon to enjoy some of the last days of summer under one of the many shade trees in the park. Brandon and Phillip also showed up, along with most of the town. The gang saw some classmates they had lost touch with over the summer.

After constructing the most awesome ice cream sundae that any ice cream connoisseur would be proud of, Nate settled against the trunk of a giant oak tree with his friends. Brandon and Phillip joined them. The conversation drifted back to all the unexplainable events in the video game.

Dion said that he spent several evenings after working at the paper drive trying to get the old *Commodore 64* to come back to life.

"It was rather frustrating," he said. "I even removed the back cover to see if anything was wrong. It looked like the plug was in good shape, so it should have been getting power, but it would not turn on. The Datasette, on the other hand, seemed to be working fine on its own."

As the group described all the strange things that happened in the *Scavenger Hunt* game, Brandon was as perplexed as they were. Phillip, usually quiet, just sat there, showing minimal reaction.

Finally, after going through the entire game, describing all the unexplainable graphics and uncanny coincidences, Phillip burst into laughter. Victor thought that maybe he had not been listening and finally just caught the gravity of what was being said.

Phillip responded saying, "I have a story that I want to share with all of you. My mother is a nurse. She often provided in-home care for the old man who lived in the mansion on top of the hill. Sometimes, when she needed extra physical support to move him around, I would go and help her. The days at the mansion would grow long. I had taken notice of the old man's briefcase and his outdated computer.

"One day," he continued, "I asked him if I could play with it, and he happily obliged. I played the original *Scavenger Hunt* game on the old machine several times. Then, I started teaching myself Basic 2, the programming language of the *Commodore 64*. Over time, I began to modify the game with current events and graphics, especially those I picked up from last year's school play and the most recent stories from your trip up Majestic Mountain."

He went on to say, "I had been working on this for months whenever I was at the mansion with Mom. We went there daily toward the end, so I had lots of time to program. There were originally two keys to the briefcase. I usually carried one with me and left the other at the mansion with the briefcase just in case I forgot mine."

Dion interjected, "Well then, how did a key end up under the waterfalls at Majestic Mountain?"

Phillip explained, "As a graduating senior, we finished school a week before the lower grades. Like several others, my class had our class picture taken under the falls at the base of Majestic Mountain. Being taller than most of my classmates, I was in the back row. The evening after the class photo, I noticed the key to the briefcase in my pocket was missing. I looked around for it but never found it. I remember that a couple of taller students and I changed positions several times during that photo shoot, trying to get the best shot. It must have fallen out of my pocket during the picture-taking session."

"So, you mean the key behind the falls had only been there for about a week?" Dion asked.

Phillip said, "Yes, that's right. I started carrying the second key after having lost the first one." He reached into his pocket and pulled out a key that matched Dion's key exactly.

Victor asked, "So, did you program all those new modern things into the original *Scavenger Hunt* game?"

"Yeah, I did," Phillip smiled.

"Well, why didn't you attempt to get the computer from Mr. and Mrs. Martinez after they purchased the mansion?" asked Victor.

"You know, I was planning to do just that, but they are never home. I have not been able to catch up with them." Phillip recalled, "I always left the briefcase in the downstairs living room to not disturb the old man upstairs. The new owners could not open the briefcase since we had the keys. They must have moved it to the attic, not knowing what was inside, figuring it would be disposed of with the rest of the old man's possessions."

Lucia remembered that Nate had noted the last date the computer was used. She said to Phillip somewhat skeptically, "The computer had not even been turned on since January 9, 1988, before we got hold of it. How is it possible that you are behind the mysterious *Scavenger Hunt*?"

"Why do you think the computer has not been used since then?" Phillip asked.

Lucia replied, "Because that is the date on the screen when we turned it on."

Phillip smiled again and explained, "That is just the date the operating system was installed. It is not a calendar keeping track of the last time the computer was used or the current date, for that matter. It is not as advanced as a modern computer. Besides, the game information is all on the Datasette and not directly inside the computer. The computer simply executes the instructions from the Datasette."

Lucia seemed satisfied with Phillip's explanation.

Then Kim asked, "Did you ever see a copy of the manuscript for our play at the mansion?"

Phillip looked puzzled. "No, why would the manuscript be at the old man's house?"

Kim told Phillip and Brandon that she had seen the manuscript the day before their last day of work at the mansion, up in the attic.

"There was no time to read it," she said. "There was an additional section—a continuation of the story in the back."

"Yes, I saw it too," Nate said.

Kim pressed Phillip, "If you did not know that there was more to *The Script*… how did you know to feature an extended version of *The Script* at the bookstore in *Scavenger Hunt?*"

Phillip shrugged. "It was just a coincidence, I guess. I was just trying to make the game more interesting. I had no idea that there was additional material beyond what was in your school play."

"We found something else from that copy in the attic. It was signed by Arthur Herring," said Kim.

Everyone knew Arthur. After all, he had been a beloved bus driver for years.

Brandon shook his head. "No. There is no way Arthur wrote that manuscript."

Nate said, "Well, his name was on it. Kim and I both saw the document."

"I never once saw a manuscript of any kind at the mansion," Phillip said. "Where is the one you saw now?"

Kim said, "We don't know. When we returned to the attic the next day, it was gone."

Brandon, looking surprised, said, "That is very strange, indeed."

Kim explained, "That was the reason we started the paper drive. We thought we could locate a copy if we collected all the unwanted paper around town. Of course, we knew that we would also be helping the town and the environment."

Phillip said, "Well, I am surprised that a copy never appeared. I hope you find one. I am rather curious now myself, knowing this background."

15

THE BONFIRE

The school had arranged for an end-of-summer bonfire for all the students returning to the tenth grade. It was a way for everyone to get reacquainted with the friends they had not seen over the summer. Everyone was super excited for Friday evening. They were particularly looking forward to sharing their summer experiences, and who had a better summer experience than the Sharefield Gang?

The group arrived at the site of the bonfire before dark. All the wood set aside for the fire was still soaking wet from the heavy rain the day before; it had been a particularly rainy summer in Sharefield that year.

Phillip, along with several of the parents, oversaw the fire. Brandon was also there to help. Phillip assembled a small pile of sticks and tried to light them, but the wood was too wet; it smoked like a coal-powered locomotive but would not catch fire.

The sun was going down as more students arrived. The smell of smoldering wood in the air was rather pleasant to Nate. It reminded him of his family's fires at home in their fireplace over the winter months. The whiff in the air brought back feelings of warmth and security.

Anthony heard someone yell, "We need some paper to start this fire!"

Anthony said sarcastically, "Well, I know where you can find some of that!"

The Sharefield Gang all laughed.

Brandon laughed, too, as he jumped in his car and headed for the warehouse. It was not far away and open late that evening for operations. All the paper from the drive was stored inside. The next week, it was to be sent for recycling. As Brandon walked in, he spotted two large boxes of paper next to all the bundled pallets ready for shipment.

Perhaps someone had left some extra paper behind after the paper drive officially ended, he thought. Brandon hastily grabbed the boxes and returned to the bonfire site.

The wet sticks were still smoldering but refusing to blaze into an open fire. It was almost dark, and everyone was waiting for the event to get going, especially since it was a bit cool that evening, thanks to all the rain. Nate watched as Anthony tried to fan the fire with a leafy branch, almost as if he were paying homage to it. Still, nothing happened. The group either sat down or roamed around in lowkey disappointment.

As soon as Brandon arrived back at the sight, he started throwing paper onto the smoking pile of wet sticks. Instantly, it burst into flames. Brandon, Phillip, and the others in charge started adding more sticks and paper to the flames as the fire began to rage. Brandon grabbed the box with the last stack of paper in the bottom and hurled it into the fire. Just as the paper flew out of the box, his eye caught the writing on the cover sheet of the stack. It read *The Script.*

He yelled, "There it is! That's it, *The Script!*"

Everyone looked at him skeptically as he began trying to reach into the flame blazing hot by then. It was too late. The manuscript had turned to ashes in a flash as he and everyone else watched.

In a somber voice, Brandon explained, "I got these boxes of paper from a separate pile at the warehouse. They were not on the pallets. They must have been left there by someone after the paper drive was over. I don't believe anyone had a closer look at what was in this box. Now, it is ashes."

What a sad situation! The manuscript that the gang had been searching for over the past couple of weeks got mistakenly burned up in the bonfire. The friends all had long faces of despair.

Then Kim cheered everyone up. "The manuscript I saw in the mansion's attic had been professionally printed."

The Sharefield Gang had learned a lot about the various types of printing over the past couple of weeks while sifting through documents, books, newspapers, and the like.

"Surely that could not have been the only copy of the manuscript?" she suggested. "Since we found one, there must be others. Printing companies doing this type of work rarely make just one copy. Once they get the equipment set up, they typically run multiple copies because it takes far less time to produce a document than configuring the equipment specifically for the job. Don't worry, guys; I believe we'll find another copy soon enough."

It worked. They all looked relatively more cheery than they did a minute ago. Kim had a knack for making others feel better.

As darkness fell, wood added to the fire, making it quickly grow in intensity. This was the perfect atmosphere for the students to share adventures and even unexplainable stories from the summer with their classmates. The teachers encouraged students to tell what happened during the summer months and explain what they learned from the experiences.

Everyone was eager to share in the excitement, but no one wanted to go first. That is, except for Kim. She had no problem taking charge and moving things forward. She was a natural leader.

She began by discussing her baseball season and how well her team performed. "It was really cool when we were presented the trophy at the end of the season." She made a special point of crediting the entire team for their ability to work together.

Lucia said, "Everyone respected Kim because she helped each player understand their weaknesses in a way that made them feel valued and able to improve."

Kim smiled modestly and said, "This summer's baseball experience made me realize that many things in life are a team effort. You have to start with a set of defined goals everyone understands and then work together to achieve them."

She would tell her teammates, "We will have a winning season!"

She meant what she had said. She always worked hard at practice and led by example.

"After losing our first game, we never looked back and went undefeated the rest of the season."

Victor added, "I watched a couple of the games. The team was most impressive."

As the fire raged in the darkness, it felt like the mood was set for scary haunted mansion stories, but that was not the topic for this fireside discussion.

Everyone was committed to keeping it real as they shared their summer experiences. There was a strong desire to share and a burning curiosity to learn what their friends had been up to over the past months. As the fire blazed, it contrasted against the flickering shadows of familiar faces in the darkness that put everyone at ease with a sense of anonymity and reserved judgment.

Kim proceeded to tell the class about the job the Sharefield Gang accepted to clean up the old mansion on the hill. Everyone at school knew them as the 'Sharefield Gang.' As she spoke, Dion felt proud to be a part of it.

She told of how she saw the *Help Wanted* notice to clean the old mansion and how the gang agreed to take on the project.

Nate said, "I remember how Kim also suggested we participate in last year's school play. Afterward, we were grateful. It was a rewarding experience. It is amazing what can be accomplished through teamwork. The paper drive we just finished is another relevant example."

"A lot of things happened this summer that were not as they appeared to be," said Kim.

She told of how the square crack in the hallway of the mansion was a doorway to the attic. Everyone was intrigued when she said she and her friends had found a copy of *The Script*.

"Did our bus driver write it?" one of the students asked.

Another student remarked that Arthur would be the last person you would expect to write a manuscript.

Victor said, "It is important not to judge too quickly because things are often not as they appear to be. Even though we don't have a copy of *The Script* to share with you, another might turn up one day."

Nate said, "I wonder what the extra sections are about."

Everyone was curious to talk to Arthur when they returned to school.

"Maybe he will finally have some answers," offered one of the students.

"Most definitely," nodded Victor.

Then Nate started, "If there is one thing I learned this summer, it is to value the group's collective wisdom. You know, we each found reading material of interest during the paper drive. Diversity makes the world go around."

After Nate finished speaking, there was talk about vacations that various students had taken with their parents. Several students relayed experiences at the national parks that sounded amazing. The descriptions of these natural wonders made everyone want to visit them for themselves.

Then, it was Anthony's turn. Everyone in town knew of the boys' journey up Majestic Mountain by this time.

"Let me fill you in on some details you may not have heard from my perspective." He started by recounting the events on the climb to the summit.

"I learned that being wrong was nothing to be ashamed of. Failure always teaches us something. Often, it is a stepping stone to success. Even though we could not build a raft at the flooded bridge that would take us across the lake, we could construct a catamaran that would have successfully taken our cell phones across if it had not been for the tree that fell into the water."

Victor interjected, "Sometimes the difference between success and failure is very small."

Anthony went on to say that he believed that problem-solving was a skill that could be improved upon with practice, just like baseball.

"Like the spider that meticulously crafted the perfect web that we admired on the mountain, we can also learn by *doing*. Problem-solving is just another skill we should learn as we grow up."

One of the girls in the class asked, "Well, how do you practice something that you do not know how to practice? Baseball has rules, and there are drills that you can perform to improve your skill, but problem-solving appears to be haphazard."

"Maybe it depends on the situation," Anthony said. "You make a good point, but I am convinced there may be techniques we can practice and rules that we can follow that will help us improve, just like baseball drills. I know this sounds a little funny, but I have learned things this summer that we may all be able to apply."

Dion could hardly hold back his words. He agreed entirely with Anthony and wanted to share his thoughts. "Anthony is correct. We need to embrace creativity as a lifestyle. We need to learn and experience many different things. This takes an open mind and a strong dose of courage. I have found that I must remain objective, even when it is so easy to follow others' beliefs. Sometimes, I convince myself something is true because I want it to be or think it should be."

He continued, "It's a challenge to live with uncertainty. I mean, it is scary when all the pieces of the jigsaw puzzle don't seem to fit together exactly as you would expect. Trying to assimilate multiple parts of an idea leads to many dead ends and sometimes agonizing frustration, but it has its rewards. Like using a shoestring around the pipe to make a modified wind chime. Like using belts with that same pipe to climb a cliff. Like observing the image in the Tree of Wisdom that helped us open the jar of peaches. Often, events from one experience relate to another. You have to experience the tension of *what next* to find it."

Victor nodded and added, "Yes, this is true in general, but it is like saying you win the baseball game by scoring runs. The question is, how do you score runs in the first place? A set of rules and applicable techniques must allow it to happen. Whether you are scoring runs, solving problems, or creating something new."

"Well, I know of one," Anthony said. "You need to put your ego aside. On the mountain, I made that silly hat with Tupperware and a paper plate to keep the glaring sun out of my eyes. Everyone laughed at me, but that hat served a valuable purpose."

"You know, Anthony," Nate told his friends, "Even though I was laughing at you, I was wishing I had one of those hats for myself because the sun was so intense that day."

So far, Lucia had been quiet throughout the discussion. Then, she revealed she had a unique approach to problem-solving.

"As crazy as it sounds, I become a particle inside the problem and travel around with it. I feel the physical effects, such as temperature or pressure, just like a small particle might feel. This technique provides me with tremendous insight. Just like I did when Dion's rocket launcher didn't work, of course, you must understand the principles associated with the problem for this to be most effective."

Anthony agreed, saying, "Oh yeah, I used Lucia's technique when we were on the mountain trying to make a pipe bell to warn a bear of our presence."

"When Nate hit the pipe that Dion was holding, my ears inside the pipe were ringing, but no sound came out. It became clear as a bell that Dion's hands were adsorbing the vibration."

"Now that you mention it, my hands tingled," Dion said. "I also discovered that solving one problem often leads to another. Once we figured out how to cross the lake, we created a new problem of losing contact with Brandon and Phillip, leading to confusion. I guess one way to be an innovator is to create the problem you solve."

Everybody laughed, but there was a grain of truth in Dion's statement. One of the students remarked, "I guess trying new things can be like that."

Dion went on to say, "Remaining optimistic when faced with a challenge is often half of the solution. Just believing that a solution is possible can lead to one, even if something seems impossible when you first look at it. Usually, when I get comfortable with a problem from all angles, I see a path, realizing it is not impossible."

"Sometimes it helps to act out a situation before you do it," Victor explained. "By visualizing ahead of time, you can gain insight, calm your nerves, and remember what's important. This is what I did before we started our mountain adventure. I wonder if that monarch butterfly somehow does something like that before it migrates?"

"Yes, but it can be a bit scary," said Lucia. "Honestly, I didn't want to return to the mansion's attic on the last day. I just wanted to let things be. Sometimes, you must feel the fear and do it anyway. We all need to learn to live with the fear of a clean sheet of paper and what might be drawn on it. It can be a bit intimidating."

She continued, "Like when we were building the mixed-up jigsaw puzzles. When we first started combining parts from the different puzzles, it made no sense. It all seemed so random. But as we collaborated, putting pieces here and there, we were able to make some sense of the chaos. If I do say so myself, the resulting masterpieces were very satisfying and rather funny. I loved the modern sailboat floating around in the castle moat."

With a chuckle, Kim added, "The Statue of Liberty on a yacht with a medieval drawbridge leading nowhere wasn't bad, either."

Their classmates all found that entertaining and laughed along in agreement.

Next, Nate took a turn. "I think it is important to do your homework so you know all you can about a subject before jumping into problem-solving; that is, if it is not an emergency, and you have the time to do the research. It rounds things out, so you do not need to reinvent the wheel. We can rely on what others have learned before us. Before our journey up the mountain, we relied on Brandon's and Phillip's experiences. They spent much time on that mountain and knew it well."

Victor said, "I learned that intuition can be valuable on its own, but combined with knowledge, it becomes a winning combination."

Nate agreed. "I don't think you can always rely just on intuition. You might fool yourself into believing something you do not know is true. When we were near the top of the mountain and decided to take the straight path, it was not the direction shown on the map. Sure, the geese were flying in a 'V' formation in that direction, but we could not base our decision on that coincidence. But we could see the top of the mountain ahead of us, so we had good reason for our choice. Had we gone on the other path, I don't know how things might have turned out."

Anthony commented, "It blew me away when Dion re-defined the problem of the strong wind that prevented us from sleeping in our tents. There is no way that they would stand up against that strong wind. Instead of sleeping inside our tents, he thought of a way for us to sleep on top of them. Thinking about opposites and redefining a problem altogether is a particularly good thing to know how to do. I didn't realize my tent cot would be so comfortable. I learned not to judge too quickly and to keep an open mind. In the end, it is the data, or in this case, our good night's sleep, which spoke for itself."

Other students shared comparable stories of solving problems by thinking in the opposite direction or defining a problem differently. Everyone agreed that this was a powerful tool they should all remember.

"I think it is good to be organized," said Victor. "I learned the value of listing things to take on our mountain adventure. It was important to me. I prioritized everything and checked items off as they were accomplished."

Dion smiled at his friend. "You did a great job, Victor. We would have been in trouble if you had not ensured we were well prepared."

"There may be techniques for putting a list together in the first place," said Nate. "Maybe the first thing one needs to do is to let a problem get under your skin. What I mean by that is you let the problem set in the back of your mind and come to the surface occasionally. The way it works for me, I think about it for a little while each time this happens and then move on to something else. Often, I am a bit frustrated because I couldn't resolve it at the time. I have heard people call this 'the incubation period,' but I think of it more as just getting acquainted with a challenge and all its parts."

Nate continued, "I'll tell you the secret of something I learned this summer. If you allow yourself to do this for a while with a problem, suddenly, a time will come when you might experience a burst of creativity almost like magic. It's important to recognize these periods of insight. It's easy to ignore them, but that is a mistake. I focus on the creative brain and let thoughts flow freely. Often, they come so quickly that I tend to forget them, like a passing swarm of insects in flight. It can be like trying to get a drink of water from a fire hose. It really helps to write everything down on the spot. It is funny because things that were unresolved in my brain start to make sense as the list gets longer and more complete.

"The most advantageous way for me to amplify these periods of creativity is to remove all other distractions and combine the session with simple and repetitive physical activity. Maybe I will go for a walk or a bike ride. Before our trip up Majestic Mountain, I did just that. There, in the quiet of Sharefield Park, I walked along and came up with a list of rules for us to follow on our journey to ensure enjoyment and safety."

Listening to all the students, Phillip commented, "Wow, this is a lot of heavy thoughts for a bonfire."

Dion interjected, "Well, now that you mention it, I have done many of the same things we talked about here tonight, but I never really thought of it in this way."

Just then, Victor heard a rumbling coming from behind him. He jumped up and spun around to see what it was. In the shadow of the fire, he could see something moving in the brush that lined the bonfire sight.

"Look," he said. "There's something back there!"

Everyone stopped talking and turned in the direction he was pointing. Dion jumped up, ran to Victor's side, and said, "Where? I don't see anything."

Just then, the noise got louder. Everyone could hear the rumblings in the bushes. They were not in just one place. There were multiple sounds distributed across the entire stretch of bushes.

It was almost as if the bush was going to attack them.

16

BONFIRE SHAKEUP

Carlos, one of the parents busy tending to the fire, jumped up and yelled, "Where are these noises coming from?"

Victor and Dion pointed to the line of bushes about twenty-five yards behind them and said at the same time, "From over there."

Carlos nudged Brandon, "Come on, let's see what's going on."

The two of them started walking toward the bushes. The students all looked on in silence as the bushes shook with life.

The students tensed as they looked on at the spectacle. Suddenly, one of the bushes seemed to grow before their very eyes! Its branches extended above its leaves, then quickly moved from side to side.

One of the girls screamed at the sight of the 'monster bush.' The shrill sound of her voice caused Carlos and Brandon to jump back a step as they looked at each other in bewilderment.

Then, a herd of eight to ten deer instantly jumped through the bushes and faced Carlos and Brandon. Many of them had huge antlers that looked like tree branches. After staring for a few seconds, they all turned around, leaped over the bushes, and darted off into the darkness like bolts of lightning.

Carlos and Brandon began to laugh as Carlos said, "Ha! The bush that came alive and grew branches were the antlers of a male deer feeding on the fresh green leaves."

Everyone was relieved and shaken at what they had just experienced. True to form, Anthony put everyone at ease by saying, "Oh, dear, you scared us! Carlos and Brandon were about to ambush your antlers. Good thing you came out of the brush then made off in a rush."

The teachers thanked Carlos and Brandon for their bravery in standing up to the 'monster.' They suggested that everyone get back to the lively discussion of events that took place over this summer.

Once again eager to take the lead, Kim said, "The things we have been discussing here tonight apply to all sorts of creative thought, even dealing with social situations. I have realized that if I try to consider how others might react to me in advance, I can think of ways to talk with them so they will better understand me."

As soon as she spoke up, the conversation comfortably returned to what it was before the scare.

"I think there's another step after all the pieces are on the table," Nate said. "Once an extensive list of important things is assembled, it's prudent to cross off the unnecessary. Simple things are easier to understand, explain, and use.

"Here is something I have thought about since returning from Majestic Mountain," he continued. "Solving problems is like climbing a tree to get the fruit at the top. If the tree is dense with leaves and branches, you can't see the top from the trunk, so you start climbing. You go off on one branch and realize it is a dead end, so you retrace your steps and pick another branch, but then you know you cannot climb from there either because the next branches are too hard to reach. So, you return to the main branch and try a different direction.

"Sooner or later, you reach the top and grab the fruit. The next time you go to climb the tree, you remember, almost exactly, which branches worked on your way up the first time, so you get to the top quicker. This is a simplified solution. The trick is to minimize the detours along the way the first time up the tree."

Anthony agreed. "It's like what I saw in the stream below the cliff early that morning on Majestic Mountain. Almost instinctively, the water knew how to curve around the rocks in advance and run downhill with the least effort. Somehow, it knew how to take the path of least resistance. Maybe long ago, the first time the water flowed down that riverbed, it figured out how to fail fast and move on, setting up patterns that directed the water upstream which way to go."

Then Victor interrupted, "But a riverbed does not stay the same. Each time a rock is moved, the water must redirect itself to the new path of least resistance. Rather amazing, I would say."

Nate nodded and commented, "After several failed attempts to cross the Wandering River, I finally decided to walk into the water, only to discover it wasn't very deep. We were ignoring the simple solution, the path of least resistance. Although, something was gained from the earlier attempts to build a raft. That is often the case. If there is time for planning, it is best to list the important things, practical solutions, and related information, then combine and eliminate pieces to simplify the list into the most basic possible."

Anthony said, "That is fine if you happen to know enough to simplify the list in the first place. I learned that you have to be proactive. When faced with a problem and no clear direction, you must choose a path and see where it leads. On the mountain, our bear drum led to the pipe bell. We didn't think of it first, only after making a failed drum. Sometimes, when you get stumped with a partially hollowed-out log, you should retrace previous drumbeats."

Victor interjected with the story of the video game they played on the old Commodore 64. "We had to go back to the haunted mansion a second time to find the storage shed beside the old mansion. Retracing our steps allowed us to solve the puzzle and win the game."

Everyone at the campfire thought it funny that the Sharefield Gang got caught up in Phillip's computer project, thinking it was mysterious. It was kind of embarrassing.

Nate came to the gang's defense. "If you had been there playing the game with us and experienced some of those spooky coincidences, you'd have been as freaked out as we were."

"Another thing I learned this summer is that you cannot rest on a previous success," said Victor. "If you want to make creativity your lifestyle, you must continue challenging yourself and muster the courage to take on new adventures. If we had not embraced Kim's idea to clean up that old mansion, we would have never found that old computer in the first place."

Kim smiled, "I think we do our best when we're having fun. It helps to laugh and find humor in a situation. It relieves stress and helps me relax, even when I'm doing something hard. Creativity is a combination of random luck and circumstances, so unless you're in the mood to catch it, you can miss it altogether. Looking back, the gang had some fun solving our challenges this summer."

"Some things still bother me," Anthony frowned. "There were just too many unexplainable happenings this summer. We learned a bit about statistics in school last year, so I understand that some things appear random, but with enough examples, you can begin to detect patterns. After playing the video game on that old computer for a while, I knew there had to be an explanation. However, I must admit that it was very entertaining and creepy as we worked through it. Not everything is like that."

"Yes, I agree with you," Dion said. "Statistics aside, some strange things happened this summer are not easily explained, and I am having a hard time believing they were all just a coincidence. It's almost like there is some mysticism at play here."

Kim asked Dion, "What was the strangest thing that happened to you this summer?"

Dion thought for a moment. "Well, maybe I can accept that the cloud we saw that looked like a bear was just our imagination. It may have come from remembering how Brandon talked to us about safety from animals before our trip. I can almost believe that the image we saw in the Tree of Knowledge resembled a bicycle. Victor's insight used that vague image to figure out that something like a sprocket and chain could open the jar of peaches. From there, we realized that his corduroy hat would do the trick. Perhaps he had a picture of a bicycle in the back of his mind when he looked at the jar of peaches. We often carry unrelated things in our heads that become useful later.

"However," Dion continued, "the one thing that bothers me the most is that my compass pointed to the straight path as north near the top of Majestic Mountain. The map we had from Brandon clearly showed that the path to our right was north. How did a physical object, the compass in my hand, point us in that direction? It was pointing to the west, and yet the compass read north. That had to be magic!"

"You make a good point," Anthony said. "Maybe there are some other forces at play here. We need to open the *Case of the Confused Compass.*"

Phillip looked very puzzled because he had no idea what was going on. "It seems to me that there must be an explanation. Let's retrace the event. Dion, what did you do first?"

Dion shrugged. "I didn't do anything special. I pulled the compass out of my pocket, opened the case, and looked at it. The needle pointed straight ahead, reading due north."

Phillip pressed Dion a little more, determined to find a logical explanation, "Where did you hold the compass?"

"At my side, next to the pocket I had taken it out of."

Nate asked, "What difference does that make?"

Phillip looked as though his head was spinning like a compass needle. Then he asked Dion, "Did you have anything else in that pocket?"

"Just my pocketknife."

Phillip had a gleam in his eye. He explained, "A compass works by pointing the needle toward the Earth's magnetic field due north. If there is a stronger magnetic field in the vicinity, it will redirect the needle of the compass. Were there any magnets close by?"

"That's it!" Dion exclaimed. "My pocketknife has a magnetic latch to hold the blade in place, either open or closed. Since I held the compass next to my pocket, the needle may have been influenced by the magnet in my pocketknife."

Everyone cheered. One mystery was solved.

Phillip went on to say, "This happens frequently. Throughout history, things that cannot be explained have been considered magic. Then, sometime in the future, science explains it. Then, the cycle continues for another unexplained mystery. For example, people used to think of the planets as mystical entities and invented all sorts of stories around their behavior. It was believed that all the planets and stars orbit the Earth. It was not till the time of Galileo and his telescope that we learned that the planets, including Earth, orbit the sun.

"Similarly, it was long believed that electrons were like little balls that orbit the nucleus of an atom. It has been shown in more recent times that this is not correct. We still don't understand many things, and maybe we never will. This is what makes discovery and problem-solving so exciting. It is our human nature to explore and to create."

With that, one of the teachers said, "This concludes our enlightening bonfire discussion. It is getting late. Thank you all for attending."

As the gang packed up to leave, they had on their minds the many strange happenings from the summer. Science is relevant, but the Sharefield Gang had witnessed some unexplained things that summer that they hoped to resolve in the following school year, and before they did so, the other schoolmates didn't need to know about them.

School would be starting in just a week. The first order of business was to approach Arthur to find out what he knew about *The Script*. Did he write it? What were the additions that the Sharefield Gang had not had the chance to read? Could they help explain the strange coincidences experienced over the past summer?

17

BACK TO SCHOOL

All these questions were crucial, indeed, but the gang was also eager to get back into the school routine. The very first day, as they loaded onto the bus, they looked at Arthur in a new light. No one told him about *The Script* on the way to school. They wanted the time to be right to broach the subject.

That afternoon, on their way home, Kim sat in the first row across from Arthur. He started his route once everyone was loaded onto the bus and situated. He had been the school's bus driver for years and knew most students by their first names. Kim leaned toward Arthur as if to say something.

Everyone sitting behind her saw that she was going to speak with him. Typically, the students talked among themselves all the way home as Arthur drove silently. He was a kind gentleman, but he pretty much kept to himself. As Kim began to speak to Arthur, the bus became silent in an instant.

Everyone wanted to hear the conversation.

Welp! Maybe this wasn't the best time to talk about it, but Kim couldn't help herself for once.

She started by saying, "It is nice to see you again, Arthur. We've had an exciting summer full of new experiences."

"That's good," Arthur grunted.

She continued, "Many things have happened since we ended the last school year with our school play. It was a good performance and fun for all of us. Did you hear about it?"

Arthur kept his eyes on the road and just nodded.

Then Kim said, "You know, that play was supposedly written by a local author who has remained anonymous."

He agreed, saying, "Yes, I heard that, too."

By this time, everyone sitting behind Kim was straining to hear every word over the background road noise.

Finally, Kim asked Arthur, "Do you have any idea who might have written *The Script*?"

Arthur looked away from the road instantly and gave Kim a rather blank look.

She pressed on, "You know, there is some suspicion… that perhaps, you wrote *The Script*."

Arthur laughed immediately. "What makes you think that?"

Kim did not want to put Arthur on the spot and tell him she had seen his name on a copy of *The Script*. No one blamed her for that. She didn't even want to let him know that she had seen a copy of it for fear he might deny ever being a part of the story everyone loved so much.

So instead, she said, "I hear that there is more to it. Apparently, there's a continuation and added detail that might explain some things that have happened. I sure hope we have the chance to discover this new material. It'd make a significant difference to me and my friends who have had the opportunity this past summer to act out, in real life, parts of the original manuscript."

"Well, I hope you continue to learn from all the experiences you have gained," said Arthur. Then he turned on his radio and began to sing along to the music.

Disappointed, Kim sat back in her chair as the chatter on the bus intensified. She was not about to give up on seeking information from Arthur, but she figured that was enough for now.

Sitting on the bus across from Kim, just behind Arthur, was a new girl whom Kim did not recognize. After speaking with Arthur, she turned to the new girl and chirped, "Hi, I'm Kim."

"Hello, I am Chelsea," replied the new girl.

"Are you new at Central High?"

"Yes, today is my first day. My dad and I just moved here because of his new job. He's a single parent."

The two girls hit it off from the very start. Chelsea was interested in theater and revealed she was a pretty darn good infielder interested in playing in Sharefield's summer girls' league.

In the days ahead, the two girls got better acquainted, talking back and forth on the bus. Kim shared the manuscript's story with Chelsea one morning after they got off the bus together before school.

Chelsea had not made many friends yet, so Kim introduced her to her classmates.

They all were friendly towards her. It looked like a new addition to the gang was on the horizon.

Chelsea told her friends what her dad had promised her once they moved and settled. She always wanted a dog, and now that she was in a new town, still trying to make friends, the dog was even more important to her.

Finally, the day had arrived. She asked Kim and Lucia if they would like to come along to the shelter that evening. They planned to adopt a new dog that its previous owner had abandoned. There were so many beautiful dogs at the shelter. It was hard to imagine that each of them had either been rescued from the streets of Sharefield or returned by owners who could no longer care for them.

Chelsea immediately fell in love with a big, white-and-brown Saint Bernard. As soon as she passed his cage, he looked up at her with the biggest dark-brown eyes. His massive head followed her as she walked by. The other two girls walking behind her took notice.

Lucia told Chelsea, "Look, this big guy won't take his eyes off you."

Chelsea turned around and came back to him. He loudly barked, and she knew this old Saint Bernard was meant for her.

She took him out of his cage and noticed he had the most enormous paws she had ever seen.

The shelter personnel, laughing, said to Chelsea, "The breed is known for having big feet."

Chelsea said, "Then we shall call him Grand Paw."

Everyone agreed that the name was quite fitting for the older Saint Bernard.

That evening, Chelsea and her dad took Grand Paw home. It didn't take the old boy long to adjust to his new home. He was a gentle and playful dog. Chelsea was overjoyed with his companionship. During the following weeks, Lucia and Kim would go to Chelsea's house after school to play with Grand Paw. He loved playing catch in the backyard with an old tennis ball he considered his own.

In the meantime, Kim was making it a habit of sitting in the front seat of the school bus every day across from Arthur. Chelsea always sat just behind him. Each day, Kim would start a conversation with Arthur. Some days, it was just a short, "Hello, how is the traffic today?"

She would always say something. Sometimes, even Chelsea would join in and ask Arthur if he was interested in theater.

Kim was the last student to get off the bus on Arthur's route. Eventually, the two of them began having exciting conversations on the way home after the other students had left the bus. Kim realized Arthur had accumulated a lifetime of knowledge on various subjects. All of which she found pretty interesting.

In fact, sometimes, if she had a complicated homework assignment, she would ask Arthur for his input. He always had something of value to say, even if he did not do her work for her. Yet, through all these conversations, he never once brought up *The Script*. Kim tried to address it with him multiple times, but Arthur always managed to change the subject.

The first conversation with him about the manuscript was not at all suspicious, but now that he was intentionally jumping around the subject, she knew he was hiding something.

One day, Lucia and Kim were at Chelsea's house doing their homework together. The girls decided to take a break and play ball with Grand Paw. He loved to fetch his special tennis ball. Each girl would take turns throwing the ball to the end of Chelsea's fenced yard and watch that big, fluffy Saint Bernard charge after it with a firm resolve and return it to the feet of whoever threw it. It was great fun for all.

After playing for a while, it was time to head back inside to finish their math assignment. Chelsea threw the ball one last time on their way into the house. It was a tough throw to the edge of the yard.

As Grand Paw took off chasing after the ball, it rolled under a gap in the chain-link fence surrounding the yard. Grand Paw was determined to retrieve his special tennis ball. He stuck his huge paw under the fence and touched the ball. Unfortunately, he only pushed it farther away.

Determined, he thrust his right leg farther under the fence in a forceful attempt to tap the ball with his paw and bring it back down to the edge of the fence, where he could grasp it in his gaping mouth. He was a big, strong dog. As he shoved his leg forward, it wedged under the fence, trapping him there.

As Grand Paw struggled to free himself, his leg rubbed against the metal fence. Soon, he began to bark as the metal fence pushed against his trapped leg. The girls heard him from inside and ran out to find Grand Paw with his right leg extending under the fence, still out of reach of his ball.

Chelsea immediately began to comfort her beloved dog. Kim and Lucia, one on each side of the massive Saint Bernard, tried desperately to lift the chain-link fence far enough to free him. It was to no avail. The girls were not strong enough to lift the heavy metal fence well secured to posts on each side.

"Go call my dad. I will stay here with Grand Paw," Chelsea instructed and continued consoling her new dog.

Lucia and Kim ran back inside and called Chelsea's father. It was the middle of the afternoon. He was at work over an hour away. He said he would leave immediately and be home as soon as possible. The girls ran outside to see how Grand Paw and Chelsea were doing. The big dog rested calmly, but the girls could not stand there. They had to do something!

Kim suggested, "Let's look in the garage. Maybe we will find something there that will help us."

Inside the garage, they found a few small yard tools, a rake, and a shovel. There was also a lawnmower and hedge clippers. Then Lucia spotted pruning shears and pointed to them.

"Maybe we can cut the chain-link fence with these," she suggested.

Kim grabbed the pruning shears as the girls took off for the back of the yard. Chelsea was petting Grand Paw to keep him still. Lucia tried to cut the fence with the shears just above the dog's leg. She squeezed with both hands but could not even dent the metal fence. Then Kim wanted to try. She strained so hard that her arms began to shake, but the shears would not penetrate the thick metal fence wire.

Lucia's eyes brightened. "I have an idea! Let's get the shovel out of the garage and see if we can dig under the fence to free Grand Paw."

The girls ran back to the garage and grabbed the shovel. They placed it just to the side of the huge dog and tried to push it into the dirt. Lucia put her foot on the shovel blade and stood up on it as she held the top of the handle with both hands. The ground was so dry that the shovel would not penetrate the soil.

Kim said, "Maybe you can hold the handle and jump onto the shovel blade with both feet to apply more force against the ground?"

Lucia tried to do just that, but the shovel did not budge as one of Lucia's feet slid off the top of the blade to one side.

Kim remembered the conversations that night at the bonfire before school started.

She thought, *In this situation, I need to stay calm, be optimistic, and remain open to all possibilities.*

She imagined herself as a miniature superhuman under the fence, lifting it off Grand Paw's leg.

"We need to find a way to be strong," she huffed.

Chelsea thought she meant that they had to remain emotionally calm and agreed, saying, "Right, let's not panic."

"Yes," said Kim. "Let's not panic, but let's also find a way to be physically strong enough to lift this fence."

"How are we going to do that?" Lucia frowned. "We can't just jack it up."

That got Kim's mind working. She remembered that often, comments from one person trigger new thoughts in another. "Lucia, you're a genius!"

Lucia looked more puzzled than before. "Thank you...?"

"We need a jack!" Kim explained.

"Oh!" Lucia exclaimed.

The two friends ran back to the garage to look for a jack. They knew it was a long shot, but it was worth trying. Unfortunately, there was nothing in the garage that even resembled one.

Don't give up. There must be a solution, Kim thought. She asked aloud, "How does a jack work anyway?"

Lucia laughed and said, "It takes advantage of mechanical leverage by converting a long motion at a low force into a shorter motion at a greater force. We learned all about these things called simple machines in science class."

Kim said, "Okay, we need to make something like that."

Lucia explained, "In its simplest form, a jack is like a teeter-totter with a small person on the long end and a bigger one on the short end."

The girls looked around the garage further. Then Kim spotted the rake again. She took it off the wall hook.

"I have an idea," she said. "We need to think in the reverse of digging under the fence. What if we use this rake and the shovel to pry up the fence from underneath?"

Lucia said, "It's worth a try. We must put something under the yard tools to create a pivot point near the fence. Then we can push down on the other end of the tools."

Kim grabbed the rake as they headed back out to the yard.

Chelsea gave them a thumbs-up, letting them know that Grand Paw was stable and resting calmly. By not moving around much, he put less pressure against the fence, so his leg was not in pain.

Lucia and Kim scoured the backyard for something that might work as a pivot under the garden tools to create a jack.

Chelsea asked, "What are you looking for?"

After Kim explained, Chelsea said, "My dad is building a paver patio on the side of the house. There should be a few loose bricks over there that might work."

Sure enough, Kim and Lucia found several bricks stacked next to those already set in place for the new patio. They each grabbed two bricks and returned to where they had dropped their garden tools moments earlier. The girls each set up the two bricks on top of each other, one on each side of Grand Paw. They positioned the bricks as close to the fence as possible.

Then Kim took the rake, and Lucia took the shovel. They each pushed the handle end of the tool under the fence, then raised the other end so that the shaft would sit on top of the bricks. Then, the girls backed up, grabbed the rake, and shoveled parts of the tools.

"Okay," said Kim, "on the count of three, let's push down and see if we can raise the fence high enough for Chelsea to free Grand Paw's leg from underneath the fence." Kim started to count.

"One, two, three . . ."

But Lucia's handle immediately slipped off the bricks to the side. She noticed that the other side of one of the bricks already had a chip out of it near the center. She said, "Wait a minute, let me position the chipped brick on top to better hold the shaft of the shovel in place." She set the shaft in the chipped brick area to prevent it from sliding to the side.

Kim said, "Okay, let's try again. Ready? One, two, three—push down!"

This time, the fence bent outward, away from the yard tool handles and raised slightly.

"It is working, just a little bit farther!" Chelsea groaned.

The girls pushed down harder, lowering the ends of the tools almost to the ground. This distorted the chain-link fence outward and raised it just enough for Chelsea to pull Grand Paw's leg gently and his giant paw out from under the fence. You could almost see a sigh of relief on the poor dog's face as the two girls dropped the yard tools to console him.

Just then, Chelsea's father arrived home and ran into the backyard. He examined the big shaggy dog and cooed, "I think he will be just fine. Nothing is broken." He smiled at the beloved new addition.

The three girls were relieved. They were proud of what they had accomplished and realized the power of what they had learned over the summer, especially that Friday evening at the bonfire.

Grand Paw walked toward the house, wobbling but not limping on the leg trapped under the fence. Chelsea's father commended the girls for their quick thinking and creativity.

Later, Kim and Lucia shared the entire experience with the rest of the gang. Everyone complimented them for successfully rescuing Grand Paw.

Dion was incredibly impressed. "Together, you solved a difficult problem in an emergency. That's a tricky thing to do. Most of the problems we encountered over the summer were not urgent. We had time to consider a solution, but you didn't have that luxury. Working under such pressure is a special skill that requires extreme focus. You girls are amazing!"

Chelsea, deeply moved by the experience, decided to make Grand Paw the subject of a poem for a school writing assignment.

She had long been intrigued by her ability to communicate with Grand Paw without a common language. Or maybe they did have a language of their own. It was just not the one she used to communicate with humans.

Look Up, Brown Eyes

Compassion strained with desperation,

His every move- an inspiration.

Born to serve humankind,

Our faithful friend's state of mind,

Now in pain without a tear,

His eyes reflect my face, his mirror,

What's inside that he must hide,

Just pet me softly by my side.

How do I say in your language,

That you'll go on to live and play,

Your loving friend's creative gift,

Move to free, deliberate, swift,

Stand and stretch, looking up, brown eyes,

So that we can see your heart's disguise.

In the days ahead, Kim continued speaking with Arthur on her way home from school, trying to get some information from him. She began to look forward to that brief time when she was the last person on the bus and could talk to him about subjects ranging from history to science.

The school's creative art faculty was considering what play they would produce this school year. In the back of her mind, Kim hoped the choice would continue last year's play. One that would tell the story of the extended script that she had seen just that one time in the attic of the old mansion.

One day, as Chelsea listened to Kim talking to Arthur, she mentioned the upcoming play, hoping that Arthur would say something about the continuation of *The Script*, even if he did not want to claim authorship of it.

Unfortunately, Arthur never commented on the play.

Ms. Brock, the theater director, decided on the new production. She decided to do something with a Caribbean theme that involved the descendants of pirates.

It would include native music and dancing. Sure, it would be fun, but unfortunately, it appeared that the mystery of *The Script* would remain unsolved.

The Sharefield Gang often met in the park to discuss significant events and relax. Chelsea began to join them as she was now part of the gang. The first game of the basketball season was coming up the following weekend.

Everyone was talking about this year's team and its chances for success. Eventually, the conversation drifted back to the things from the past summer that still puzzled the group.

Would the *Commodore 64* ever work again?

Is a descendant of the monarch butterfly going to return to the exact location this summer?

Would something unexplained happen in the next school production?

What was that magic key in the play for anyway?

Why did the rock it was under in the play look like the one on Majestic Mountain?

How was this key standing on edge?

They asked, and they wondered. The Sharefield Gang had solved several mysteries, but many remained, and this frustrated them a little.

Of course, they wanted answers, but nobody was willing to give it to them, especially their bus driver.

* * *

That Friday, everyone was excited about the first basketball game. The noise level on the bus ride home was deafening.

Most unexpectedly, Arthur, who usually just drove and did not say much, got out of his seat at the first stop. He stood in front of the double rows of seats, all full of singing students. He cleared his throat. Everyone went silent and looked up at him.

He announced, "After many years, I am leaving this job and will retire. Today is my last day driving your bus. You will all be missed."

Everyone looked on in shock and despair as Arthur sat back in his driver's seat, pulled the bus away from the curb, and then proceeded to drive down the street.

Along the route that day, there were many questions from the back, asking him what he planned to do next. Everyone who got off the bus that day wished him well. He just kept to his driving and did not have much else to say.

Finally, only Kim was left on the bus. She would never forget that day.

First, she said to Arthur, "I am quite surprised. What made you decide to retire? I'll miss you."

Arthur had little to say. Pulling up to Kim's stop, he opened the door, and she got off the bus. Then Arthur said, "I have something for you."

He stood up and walked to the steps at the entrance to the bus. He reached down and handed Kim a gold pen.

She no sooner looked down to admire the gift when the door to the school bus closed.

Kim wanted to say thank you to Arthur, but the bus was already pulling away from the curb. Kim looked at the bus moving into traffic. She looked back down at the pen and then up at the bus again. Somehow, Kim knew this pen was special.

18

THE NEW PLAY

The tryouts for the new school play were rapidly approaching. It was announced that the title of this year's production would be '*The Caribbean Adventure.*'

It would include music, dancing, history, and a pirate story. Ms. Brock did not have any trouble recruiting students this year. Last year's play was a rewarding experience for everyone in the gang. On the second day of tryouts, the Sharefield Gang watched as Ms. Brock walked through the main scenes of the play.

As much as they all wanted this to be a success, they had to admit, it was very sketchy. Little detail was in place. She said, "My goal right now is to give you an idea of the storyline."

As she orchestrated the various scenes with commentary and hand motions, Kim and Nate recognized the same rock from last year's play—the one under which the magic key was found. Kim pointed it out to Dion, who said, "Ms. Brock, I see that we are using the same rock that was in last year's play."

Ms. Brock replied, "Yes, I like this rock. We will use it again this year."

Then, Kim asked who wrote this year's play. Ms. Brock said that the name of the author was not being released.

"You mean, just like last year, we are not going to know the author of our play?" Kim asked.

"That is correct."

Nate said, "That rock is just like the one we saw on top of Majestic Mountain. How can that be?"

Ms. Brock was astonished. She was not aware that the boys had seen a similar rock.

Finally, she smiled and said, "Okay, I will tell you the history of this rock. I had it made specially for last year's production. When I was a young adult, before I got married, my twin brother, Jimmy, and I used to love to climb Majestic Mountain. We made it our pastime and set off up that mountain every chance we had. It became a sport for us. Each time, we would try to do it faster. Sometimes, we would compete against each other to see who could reach the summit the quickest.

"At the top, we would declare victory by being the first to claim a small orange-and-black flag that we kept hidden under a rock like this one. To us, the rock and the flag, the colors of a monarch butterfly, represented a sense of accomplishment, a job well done.

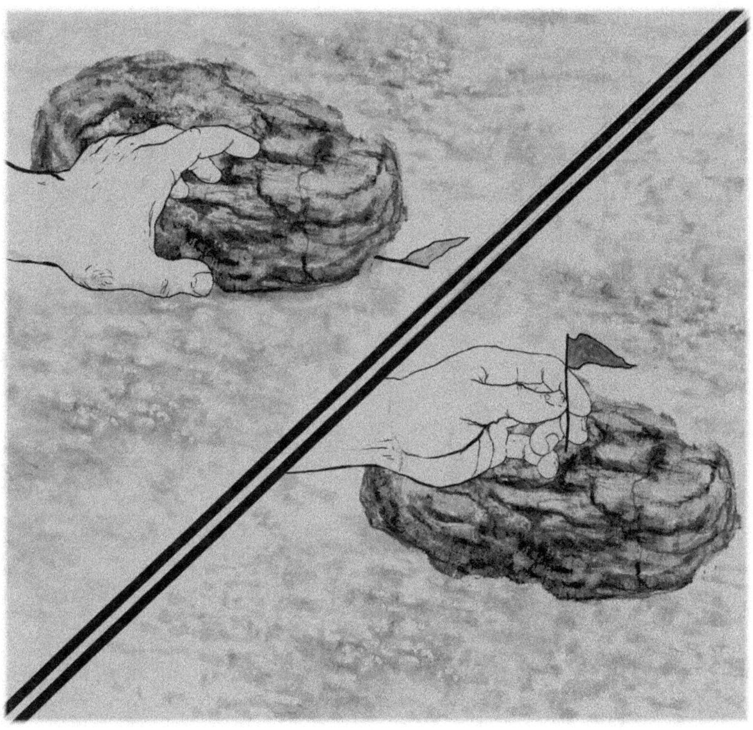

"If I were the first to the top of the mountain, I would plant the flag in the hole in the rock with the orange side pointing north for Jimmy to find when he arrived. If he were there first, he would plant the flag in the rock with the black side pointing due north for me to find upon my arrival."

Victor recalled seeing the caterpillar under the rock he overturned on the mountain. Knowing that he was facing the morning sun when he turned over the rock, he realized that the caterpillar was lying there facing south to north.

That seemed fitting, he thought.

Ms. Brock continued, "That sense of accomplishment is probably not much different than what you, Nate, and your friends felt at the top of Majestic Mountain. That rock is particularly dear to both me and my brother. Since last year's play involved an excursion up the very same Majestic Mountain, I decided to have a replica of the special rock made as a good luck charm. It's something that stands for the results of hard work."

Anthony interjected, "Then we shall call this rock, 'The Rock of Jill Brought Her.'"

"Well, that explains the rock we found on the mountain. It is still up there!" Nate exclaimed.

Remembering last year's play, Victor added, "There was a mysterious flashing of lights when the rock was turned over and the key was found. How could that have happened?"

Ms. Brock laughed. "Well, you didn't have the opportunity to meet him, but I invited Jimmy backstage for your performance. He has a bit of a dramatic side to him. After your star presentation, he confessed to me that he briefly flickered the lights a couple of times just to acknowledge that all of you were accomplishing the same thing he and I had accomplished on the mountain. You all worked incredibly hard for months to make the school play an almost flawless performance. I think he wanted to salute your joint success in his special way."

Kim had been trying to figure out who wrote *The Script* since the beginning of last summer. She now realized Ms. Brock must know more about this manuscript than everyone thought. It did not just show up at the school. Ms. Brock was in on it.

"Ms. Brock," she said, "why can't you tell us who wrote *The Script*? You must know more. I briefly saw a printed copy while working in the old mansion over the summer. I did not have a chance to read any of it, but it said Arthur Herring, our bus driver, wrote it. There were additions to the manuscript in the back that were beyond what we did in our play last year. Did Arthur, the bus driver, write the play? Is he the mystery author?"

Ms. Brock was amazed. She had no idea that anyone other than herself had seen a copy of *The Script*.

Kim said, "I asked Arthur if he wrote it, and he would not answer me."

"No, Arthur did not write the play," confirmed Ms. Brock.

"Then who did?" asked Kim.

"It was Jimmy, my brother."

Everyone was confused.

"Well," Nate said, "if your brother Jimmy wrote *The Script*, why was Arthur Herring's name on it?"

Ms. Brock smiled. "That is his name, Arthur James Herring. We always called him Jimmy to avoid confusing him with my dad."

"So, you and Jimmy are twins, and Arthur, our recently retired bus driver, is your father?" Victor questioned.

"Yes, that is correct."

Kim was flabbergasted. "Wow, after all this time, things are coming together!"

Everyone was amazed.

Then Lucia asked, "What was a copy of *The Script* doing in the attic of the old mansion? Why was it there one day and gone the next?"

"I was not going to tell you all of this. The old man who lived in the mansion was a distant uncle in our family. My older sister, Claire, has wanted to return to Sharefield for some time. After our uncle's death, she and her husband, Daniel, decided to purchase the old mansion at the auction and turn it into a bed and breakfast while they lived in the lower level."

"So, were we working to clean the old mansion for your sister?" Kim asked.

"Yes, Claire told me that you all did a fantastic job. My brother must have stopped by to see his sister at the old mansion. He probably dropped off a copy of the manuscript for her to read. He is quite proud of it, you know. It must have been put into the attic by mistake and then recovered by my sister before the disposal service arrived. I know that Claire went through the entire mansion, top to bottom, before trash removal to ensure that they kept everything they did not want to dispose of."

"This is all very interesting," said Kim. "I thought Arthur, our bus driver, wrote the manuscript."

Ms. Brock said, "Well, Jimmy is much like our father."

"I have one more question," Kim said. "What about the extra sections to *The Script* that I got a glance of that day up in the attic of the old mansion?"

Ms. Brock said, "You are really pushing me for information! I was not going to tell you all of this, but since we have opened the book, so to speak, I will continue. Jimmy originally wrote *The Script* to document the diverse plant life that flourishes on Majestic Mountain. He has a strong interest in botany. Once he got into it, he made it more of an adventure story, climbing up the mountain. Remembering our favorite rock, he included it in the story because it signifies as much to him as it does to me.

"After our early adult years of climbing the mountain, I studied theater and education while Jimmy became a botanist. He has traveled to many distant places to study various plant species. One of his favorite trips was to the Caribbean, where he fostered lasting friends with the locals, who he found quite charming. Jimmy extended his original writing of *The Script* to include an adventure in the Caribbean."

"So, this year's play is your brother's extension of *The Script!*" Lucia said.

"That is correct," smiled Ms. Brock. "It will include authentic music, dancing, and some fascinating characters, along with a few educational descriptions of the beautiful foliage of the Caribbean."

The gang all thanked Ms. Brock for sharing her story and that of her brother on the mountain, along with all the events that followed. Her explanation tightened so many of the loose ends that had been unraveling in the minds of the Sharefield Gang since the night of the school's theater production of *The Script* last spring.

It was Friday afternoon. The friends decided to meet in the park on Saturday to discuss everything they had heard from Ms. Brock. That afternoon in the park, there was a lot of lively discussion about how easy it is to misinterpret information and to be misled into believing things that are not entirely accurate. Everyone had something to say about how they felt when they learned the truth from Ms. Brock.

Many of the things they thought must be mystical had logical explanations.

Dion said, "It is like when you are a child, your imagination runs wild. You believe in fairy tales and see the world in an imaginary way. Then, as you grow up, you realize that everything is not exactly as you thought it was years before. You learn that there are logical explanations for the mysteries you experienced as a little kid. When that happens, many people flip to the opposite perspective and begin to think that everything can be explained by what they know or think they know.

"That is a shame. They have given up on their creative spirit. Maybe there is somewhere in the middle where creativity and imagination make up a world of partial ambiguity. A place where logic rules, but not all the answers are known."

Victor agreed. "It's uncomfortable to admit you don't have all the answers. It means that you don't have full control over your environment. That goes against our sense of security."

Kim interjected, "I'm feeling that right now. Why would the owner of the outdoor supply store be suspicious of Ms. Brock's brother, Jimmy? He is her twin and apparently has a lot of her same energy. She said he has traveled the world. He should be quite at home in an outdoor supply store."

Dion replied as he looked directly at Kim. "You never really know what someone is feeling inside. Sometimes their words don't always correlate directly with their actions."

"Well, if we have some answers, it's not all bad," Anthony said. "I think not having the answers to everything is good for us. It pushes us to learn, try new things, and explore. We gather nuggets of information that we can combine into something new. Creativity is really nothing more than that. If you go out on a limb and dare to think differently than everyone else, you are being creative."

Lucia grinned. "That is a good way to put it, my friend."

Everyone concurred. This was a simple way of expressing things.

Lucia said, "We didn't get an explanation from Ms. Brock for one thing that's still bothering me. What was the significance of the key in *The Script* that ended up in safe deposit box 395 at the local bank? We need to ask Ms. Brock about that the next time we meet for theater practice."

Lucia did just that the following week. Ms. Brock told her that the key had special significance in continuing *The Script*. She said we would learn more about it as Jimmy's story unfolds.

Victor asked, "How could the key stand on its edge in last year's production? It weighted a large rock on top of it."

Ms. Brock smiled and said, "When you look at the rock, you take it at face value, that is, from the top side. The underside of this rock has a groove cut in it that supports the key on its edge. In fact, it will reveal to you that the underside has a full inscription engraved on its surface. It identifies the coordinates of a place just off the coast of a small, unknown Caribbean island. Perhaps you will learn more about this place in this year's production."

Lucia pressed on, "You must tell us more about this mysterious key."

"All in due time," said Ms. Brock gently. "Maybe not having all the answers is a good thing. Perhaps what the key represents, more than anything else, is a reflection of the human spirit to unlock the mysteries of this world through our innate creativity."

"Does the key open a chest of treasures in this year's play?" asked Kim, half-hopeful.

"Well, that remains to be seen, but symbolically, it is exposing us to the treasure chest of knowledge and creativity right this very minute. We all have that spirit within us. Each of our expressions is uniquely our own, but the basic trait is universal. Those who accept their mission always to discover new things will greatly enrich their lives. The rewards are tenfold the effort if one dares to act. Adopting a lifestyle of creative thought is *The Key on Edge* that leads to all the riches of a life fulfilled."

THE END

About the Author

Michael J. Piatt lives in Cincinnati, Ohio. After a lengthy career as a technologist and inventor, he shares lessons learned through this book and those to follow in The Key Series.

If you were entertained or found value in this book, please consider leaving a review. It helps immensely.

Be on the lookout for the following books in The Key Series, as the story continues.

DISCUSSION NOTES

INTRODUCTION

The freedoms to explore, discover, redefine, and share are the gifts bundled together and labeled "creativity." This book is dedicated to techniques that can enhance these precious human qualities.

What exactly does a review of the fundamentals of creativity entail? Although it can be expressed in many ways, the actual methodology of creative thought is a topic that is generally not a part of the educational curriculum in its purest form. That is perhaps because it is more of a lifestyle than a fixed set of knowledge. It includes constructive daily habits of seeking out personally undiscovered information while maintaining an unbiased perspective and then working tirelessly to correlate newfound insights with the status quo.

This is the heart of creativity. It is both a curiosity within that drives new thoughts and an intelligence to combine those thoughts with what has come before. The creative process is illusive and generally not well understood. Many think that you either have this innate ability or you do not.

Like other human qualities, there are varying degrees of natural talent. However, consistent with any other life skill, it can be acquired and nurtured. Anyone can enhance their ability to engage in creative thought through practice if given the proper tools. One simply must be dedicated to the task and have a passion for innovation.

To help understand the difference between the basics of creative engagement and creative expression, consider an analogy to mathematics. The principles of fundamental mathematics are the tools of engagement that are then applied to solve complex real-world problems, often through an expression of creativity.

The application of basic principles to solve a problem is typically not obvious. It requires creative expression. Likewise, if someone wants to become a musician, they may first learn music theory and the mechanics of playing an instrument. One may excel at these, becoming an accomplished musician. Having the tools of engagement that can make one a great musician does not necessarily translate to a creative composer capable of bringing forth something that did not exist before. However, such knowledge and skill are a necessary first step.

Creative thought processes are a set of tools that help one to bring forth what did not exist before. They are not as definitive as mathematical principles. Hence, the results of their application are probabilistic and can be difficult to measure. The concepts may seem hard to grasp or even invalid because results can often be random.

A good basketball player does not make every shot but remains keenly aware of higher and lower percentage shots and acts on that understanding. Similarly, practicing a creative methodology on a continuous basis allows one to hone their skills and improve their creative performance. Just as one can form habits of a healthy lifestyle that have positive results, similarly, one can live a lifestyle of enhanced creativity that continues to improve over time as the skill develops.

There is rarely one fixed approach or single right answer to creative expression. Very few things are black and white. Because results appear random but are actually somewhat probabilistic, one can increase their odds or sometimes make their own luck, so to speak, through consistent behavior that is conducive to enhanced creativity.

It is important not to let the lack of direct *cause-and-effects* discourage one from continuous improvement that will result in more favorable results on average over time. Our brains are immensely powerful! We can transform our creative thinking ability with proper and repeated actions.

Creativity can be expressed in infinite forms, but the mindset of innovation is common to all. Whether one is sculpting a statue, writing a symphony, designing a high-rise building, solving a physics problem, putting together a political strategy, developing a new recipe, or evolving new ways to practice for a sporting event, the tools of engagement for each of these expressions have many common elements.

It is imperative that we equip the next generation with these life skills so that each person can reach their full creative potential in whatever endeavors they choose to pursue.

The world is changing incredibly fast. More than ever before, there is a need to pay attention to the fundamentals of creative thought. Many of the challenges the next generation will face are not yet apparent. The ability to adapt through innovation is essential.

The format for this guide includes the identification of a concept and examples from the story, followed by suggestions for further discussion. Although the examples of creative engagement in this book are expressed as simple problem-solving exercises, these tools can be extended to the broad spectrum of creative endeavors that we, as humans, are drawn to by our very nature.

1. Definition of Creativity

Description: There are numerous kinds of intelligence and expressions of creativity, just as there are different ways of quantifying intelligence. Creativity is a term that is tossed around for the innovation of a well-choreographed dance, a revolutionary electromechanical innovation, a provocative new painting, an athlete's new move, an intriguing literary work, a politician's strategy, a biochemical cure discovery, and so on.

Each is an assimilation of known information in a unique way, that together form a new discovery. The insight from that discovery is then exploited to change the way reality is perceived. Creativity had an impact by definition.

Whatever the circumstances, it is our nature as human beings to explore and find a better, or at least a different, way to do things. Often, creative expression is the culmination of inputs that spring forth from a variety of sources. Often, problem resolution is a team effort. The ability to properly combine valuable nuggets of understanding promotes the advancement of society. In terms of useful objects, the function should come first, followed by form. Form is a judgment that can change with norms. Function is steadfast.

Equally important is one's ability to discard information that is not relevant, concentrating only on what is most important in a particular circumstance. If properly simplified to the minimum requirements and nothing more, the results can be beautiful.

Book Examples: There are multiple examples of creative expression embedded throughout the book. Some are more obvious than others. The characters themselves reiterate many of them in discussions around the bonfire.

Here are a few examples:

Kim was able to convince her friends to take part in the school play by appealing to their sense of loyalty.

Anthony combined a paper plate with a Tupperware bowl to make a cap that shielded him from the sun.

Dion made sleeping cots from branches and the boys' tents, then stretched them across a ravine to shield the boys from the wind.

Nate defined the set of rules the boys would follow on their expedition up Majestic Mountain.

Victor figured out how to open the jar of peaches with his corduroy hat.

Lucia identified the wiring problem with Dion's rocket launcher.

Points of Discussion: To reach the best solution, one must put one's ego aside and focus on the approach. This can be an awkward thing to do. It requires discipline and honest assessment. When has your refusal to evaluate an idea objectively stood in the way of creative expression? When was an irrelevant idea discarded because it was impeding progress toward a solution? If Victor was intent on using his jacket to make a drumhead. That failed attempt may have prevented the gang from ever coming up with a pipe bell.

Many ideas are the result of collective thinking. Filtering ideas becomes an important exercise in the quest for a solution. This can be contentious because there is often more than one valid approach to a creative endeavor. When have you wrestled with more than one approach to a creative exercise?

2. Embracing Creativity as a Lifestyle

Description: The human mind is continuously occupied with a stream of thoughts. Studies have shown that many of these thoughts are a repeat of earlier ones. This can be a good thing. It allows us to form habits that remove the mental burden of performing repetitive tasks. If one ever questions the value of a well-rehearsed habit, try doing something new for the first time and appreciate how much concentration it requires.

A creative lifestyle demands that one make a conscious effort to learn and do new things on a regular basis, thereby moving out of their comfort zone. It is sometimes referred to as 'living with the intimidation of a clean sheet of paper.' It is difficult, plain, and simple. One needs to continually challenge themselves to grow. It means learning a variety of different things and assimilating information from one area into another.

To live this lifestyle, one must be observant, willing to ask questions and seek out information while not judging too quickly. It takes courage. It takes patience. Likewise, it takes dedication. It takes a constant focus on information whose relevance may not be immediately identifiable, along with the understanding that it may be randomly applicable in the right situation sometime in the future. It is well-established that the brain is influenced by repeated behavior. If one wants to be more inclined to creativity, they practice it through tools of engagement.

As information is gained, it should constantly be compared, contrasted, and fit into what is already known in hopes of finding a new synergistic match. Remaining cognizant of the possible integration of many thoughts is a daunting task that can be very tiring. Fortunately, it is something one can turn on and off in one's head and exercise at varying degrees, depending on the situation. Emotion drives discovery. If there is passion, the task can be effortless. Create within the subject matter you love.

Book Examples: The book describes ways of obtaining and assimilating information from one context to another to create something new.

The transformation of the vision of a wind chime on a porch into a pipe bell that would warn a bear of the presence of humans is one such example. Using a hat to open a jar of peaches is another. Figuring out that the handles of a rake and shovel could be used to make a jack to free a Saint Bernard is yet a third example.

Points of Discussion: Can you trace the origin of thought in an existing creative work? Have you ever combined unrelated parts to create something new?

Creativity builds upon itself as the person, or the entire society, advances. As a deeper understanding is developed, more information becomes accessible. The more abundant the resources available to combine with the status quo, the better the chances of their integration into something new.

The fundamentals of creativity span all genres of art, science, and social behavior. One can improve their creativity in any area of interest by practicing a lifestyle of seeking out information of known relevance and sometimes unknown relevance while remaining ever vigilant of the possibility of combining it with the current state to create what did not exist before.

How has formal training supported creativity in a specific discipline? What is missing from formal training in the creative process?

3. Work Hard to Make It Happen

Description: It is not easy to be vigilant. The motivation to collect nuggets of information that may someday be relevant to an unknown situation is challenging. By doing so, one makes their own luck, so to speak. Calling upon experiences and information obtained somewhat randomly from the past and applying them to the situation at hand is easier said than done. When faced with a problem, one must make a concerted effort to do so.

Often, there are missing parts to a solution. Therefore, the creative mindset is more of a lifestyle than a singular event. One never knows what can be applied to a future creative endeavor. One's toolbox from which to draw is only as large as the work they have done to increase their knowledge base.

Further, it is important to have a well-articulated goal when creating something new. What is measured gets accomplished.

Like a professional actor on the stage, every day requires a star performance as a part of the task, whether inspired at the time or not. It is easy to be lazy and accept defeat too soon.

To enhance creativity, one must engage and learn as they go. Failure is a great teacher, but it should not overtake the passion to be successful. Learning to fail in small steps is a necessary, acquired skill.

One should strive to gain the most insight possible while minimizing potential negative consequences and then advance with the newfound knowledge. Quick and simple simulations of critical concerns can direct further actions most efficiently. Engagement directly into the situation is the key.

After one learns what they can through research and past experiences, they should keep the challenge front and center as they ponder a solution.

Then, let it go for a while, only to bring it back to the forefront repeatedly as time goes on. The subconscious mind will be working in the background to sort out the confusion.

Often, there comes a time after such periods of incubation when a solution starts to formulate in one's head. This time may come suddenly and unexpectedly. It can easily be passed off as a fleeting thought and ignored. To do this is a big mistake. When one is in a creative state of mind, with seemingly new revelations coming into focus, one should take advantage of that time to explore the possibilities.

Distractions should be minimized. In addition, light, repetitive physical activity often helps to stimulate the thinking process, such as a slow, leisurely walk. Everyone is a bit different in this regard and, therefore, should develop their own unique environment for creative thought. The important thing is to recognize these heightened periods of creative activity and focus on them.

A thorough record should be kept of such sessions because inspirations may emerge as fleeting thoughts that are quickly dismissed. Often, numerous possibilities are forthcoming in a short amount of time, making documentation challenging but necessary.

Book Example: Before Nate made the trip up Majestic Mountain, he was bothered for some time about how he and his friends might get along for three days without the comforts of home. He recognized the time when the solution started to come to him, so he went for a walk, which resulted in a list of rules of conduct for the journey that his friends readily accepted. If he had not let this problem bother him so much leading up to the journey, the rules of conduct would have never emerged on their own. He was able to focus and solidify the list on a walk through Sharefield Park.

Kim and Lucia were able to fail fast and move on in their attempts to free Grand Paw's leg from the fence. They learned from each failed attempt and moved on without reservation or bias.

The goal to climb Majestic Mountain was well-defined before the journey began. Otherwise, the boys may not have been prepared, or they may have changed their objective without due cause.

Points of Discussion: Have you ever had a period of enlightenment after a nagging issue was in the back of your mind for some time? What is the best environment for you to sort out new revelations?

What challenging task have you taken on with the goal of creating something new? Was the goal well specified?

What did you learn from failure through a creative endeavor? How have you been able to fail with minimum impact and move on? When has a quick simulation provided you with insight?

4. Understanding Knowledge, Reason, and Intuition

Description: It is human nature to create what did not exist before. Yet, we really do not understand exactly how we do it.

The mind is complex. It is safe to say that creativity is somehow a mixture of accumulated knowledge, sound reasoning, intuition, and serendipity, all acting in unison to bring forth a new expression of reality in one form or another.

It may not be possible to accurately break down the contribution of each and to predict success with any degree of certainty, but there are observations worth consideration.

Knowledge is the framework about which creative thought can be built. Intuition is best trusted when knowledge and experience are well established. Otherwise, intuition is a mere wild guess that one has convinced oneself carries more weight than it should. Under these circumstances, the probabilities of success are not in its favor. However, the intuition that springs forth from the subconscious processing of information that has been thoroughly vetted is likely credible.

Many creative exercises involve sequential processes. In these situations, it is helpful to periodically retrace sequences, checking each against logic and fundamental principles.

Sometimes one does not have the luxury to acquire background information or the time for careful reasoning. Under such conditions, one should just take action in the unknown, be as observant as possible, and adjust course according to the data without any bias. Attention given to probability and statistics in such instances is most valuable.

Book Examples: Victor saw the image of a bear in the sky from Camp Y Knot prior to entering the dense forest, where Dion later spotted an actual bear.

Was this a random coincidence? Maybe, but Brandon had mentioned that bears were rarely seen on Majestic Mountain prior to the boys' expedition. The dense forest would be the most likely place for one to reside. Perhaps Victor's subconscious mind remembered Brandon's words and was processing the likelihood of an actual sighting.

While playing a video game on an old computer, the Sharefield Gang retraced their steps, visiting the mansion on the hill a second time. This time, they located the storage shed and found the next clue. Had they refused to acknowledge that they might have missed something when they were there the first time, they never would have won the game.

After trying unsuccessfully to make a raft suitable for carrying the boys across the lake at the Wandering River flooded bridge, Nate took action and started walking directly into the lake to test the waters. Often, the obvious is not apparent. It can be shielded by preconceived notions and historical bias that can overcomplicate a situation and cloud vision.

Sometimes, unpredictable things just happen. The tree falling into the lake, tipping the catamaran raft, and dumping the bag of cell phones into the water was completely unpredictable. When these things happen, it becomes necessary to objectively assess reality and take appropriate action from that point rather than consider how things could have been or should have been.

Points of Discussion: Have you ever been fooled by a misconception that was never confirmed? When did you take action and learn valuable insight? Can you recall when your intuition was correct and what may have helped your subconscious mind to reach the right conclusion? Have substantial amounts of statistically significant data ever provided you with creative insight? When has a logical analysis of processes and procedures supported your creativity? Have you ever made progress by backing up and revisiting old ideas?

5. Creative Expression and Problem-Solving Techniques

Description: There are techniques to enhance creative expression and to aid in problem-solving. One immensely powerful technique is to put oneself directly into the creative effort as a microscopic particle. By being a part of the creative initiative, removed from oneself, one can see things from a more intimate perspective. Seeing how the parts interact while remaining grounded on fundamental principles can be a very powerful technique to enhance one's insight.

Nature has developed countless ways of coping with the physical world. The more one understands its solutions, the better chance one has of applying similar techniques.

A necessary condition for problem-solving is to fully understand the root of the problem. Many times, a problem is misstated or not expressed completely. Sometimes, redefining a problem into one that is easier to solve works well. Another enormously powerful problem-solving technique is to consider the exact opposite of the current thinking.

Brainstorming by oneself or in collaboration with others can be incredibly valuable, but boundary conditions of creative expression need to be kept front and center. Otherwise, one may be misled, concentrating on things that are not directly applicable to the creative exercise at hand. While one should be aware of fixed boundary conditions, one should not enforce artificial boundaries or categorize things that are better left unsorted.

It is important not to judge people or situations too quickly. Further, one should never underestimate the value of humor in the creative process. Somehow, humor releases inhibition and promotes a more harmonious union between the conscious and the unconscious mind. It is an effective way of assimilating information from different sources and making connections that can often add value.

These methods do not guarantee success, but they can increase their probability.

Book Examples: The Sharefield Gang built three jigsaw puzzles at the same time by combining different parts from each puzzle. Inventing is a lot like this.

The girls freed Grand Paw's paw with a simple solution. They got the idea to raise the fence rather than trying to cut it or dig underneath it. Ironically, it was the shovel and rake held opposite to their intended use, with the handles forward under the fence and the tool parts up in the air, which solved the dilemma. Exploring opposites is a very powerful creative technique.

Lucia used the microscopic particle technique to help Dion figure out how to fix his rocket launcher. Anthony did the same thing to analyze the pipe bell.

Regarding the pipe bell, the problem of the bear was solved not by building a defense against the bear but by redefining the problem to make a human warning device. The boys were not going to hide from the bear or defend against it, but rather, just make their presence known.

Understanding background information about the behavior of bears was most helpful in finding a solution to the bear problem. Attempts to build a warning device were concentrated within the boundaries of the materials and the capability available.

Anthony's humorous name for the bear, "Cloud Claw, the Billowing Bear," was inspired by Victor's vision of a bear in the sky. The vision was lost due to turbulence in the sky, which triggered Nate to say, "The whispering wind blew him away."

That phrase, in turn, led Nate to recall that bears will stay away from humans if they make their presence known with loud noises. Was this all just random luck?

Not exactly. Perhaps it was the creative process at work. Metaphors and related verbal expressions of thought often facilitate creative thinking.

Creativity can be elusive, but one can tip the scales in their favor when armed with extensive background information, careful observation, living in the moment, viewing things from a different perspective, and sometimes a little humor and serendipity.

Points of Discussion: Have you ever redefined a problem so that you could solve it? Name a time that you were part of a brainstorming session. Did it veer off track into impractical approaches? How has humor helped your creativity? Has your subconscious ever triggered something that enhanced your creative pursuit? When has seemingly random luck favored your creativity?

6. MAKE LISTS

Description: Never underestimate the value of a prioritized list. One may think that a list is not necessary because they have a good memory. A list does much more than keep track of what is at hand. It summarizes a situation. A list of concerns, partial solutions, or boundary conditions defines the state of completion of a creative project. It delineates what is known and what is unknown. If properly constructed, it amplifies major concerns and helps to identify a plan of action and even offers a schedule for such. Lists used in the context of creative endeavors are a living document, subject to change, that often reveals new insights.

The advantage of such a list is that it is easy to make and modify. A list can be written out with old-fashioned pen and paper or by using a 'notes' app on a smartphone. In some cases, it may be a complex spreadsheet, depending on the situation. Consider it a stream of consciousness. It is easy to cross off irrelevant information and add new points for consideration. It is a no-pressure way to identify the state of the creative endeavor. It can be as detailed as necessary. Sometimes, single words are sufficient, and other times, more complex explanations are appropriate.

The saying 'Don't sweat the small stuff' applies. A prioritized list helps one to understand what is important and what is not.

Lists of one type or another are relevant because most creative endeavors follow a nonlinear path, with multiple parts coming together in parallel rather than in a linear and serial fashion.

Book Examples: Prior to the expedition up Majestic Mountain, Victor made a list of everything he needed to bring. One may argue that this was not an expression of creativity. However, having the list in front of him helped him decide what to put in his backpack and what to leave behind. It forced him to think through the journey in advance. Acting out an experience in one's mind before doing it has been shown to significantly increase performance.

Points of Discussion: When has a list proven valuable to you in a creative process? How often should you modify a creative list? Where have you used a list for prioritization and scheduling? How might you use a list in the future to support a creative exercise? When in the creative process is a list most relevant to you—in the beginning or near the end? Have you ever referred to a list of criteria and attempted to satisfy everything in it through one simple approach?

7. SIMPLIFYING CREATIVE EXPRESSION

Description: Often, the first solution is not the best one. An elegant solution includes all the necessary parts and no more. Making a list helps one to simplify creative expression. One should list all aspects of the result and then cross out the ones that are not necessary. A precursor to this is a good definition of the objective of the creative exercise.

A simple creative expression is easier to communicate and understand. A simple solution is also less prone to failure. Any solution is only as good as its weakest link. Sometimes, a solution or artistic expression seems to go against nature or basic principles. It is like pushing a ball uphill. Nature takes the path of least resistance. Strive to solve problems from their root cause rather than trying to cover up the symptoms. Sometimes, finding the root cause is analogous to peeling an onion to reveal the various layers below what is obvious on the surface.

An elegant expression of creativity, meaning one that fits the situation like a glove, takes advantage of naturally occurring forces, whatever they might be. Creative simplification is an acquired skill. One must review the result in their mind without any bias. Tracing through a solution often leads to extraneous parts that can be eliminated. Sometimes, the problem is redefined altogether through this process.

Book Examples: Nate's decision to walk into the lake at the flooded Wandering River Bridge was a solution simplification. Given enough time and energy, the boys may have been able to construct a raft to carry them across the lake or find another means to aid them in crossing. Attempting to walk across the lake directly was the simplest and most straightforward approach. However, it left two pieces of the problem unresolved: how would the boys protect their phones and the food that was not sealed, and how would they know if their next step on the bottom of the lake was safe, given that they could not see their feet? Each of these secondary problems was solved in a simple manner. The boys had already collected wood for a raft that they intended to build for themselves. It was a straightforward approach to convert the raft into a smaller and less demanding version that would hold their phones and open food containers. Similarly, using a branch to feel the lake bed terrain prior to taking the next step was simple and effective. Often, there is value gained from a failed effort that is applicable to the optimal solution of a creative endeavor.

Points of Discussion: When have you had a solution that was almost perfect, but there was one issue that was not resolved? Did you find a way to resolve that issue, or did you find a completely different approach that avoided the issue altogether? When were you able to remove something from a creative expression and end up with a simpler and more elegant result? When did something fail because of one small thing that was not considered fully? Have you ever come up with a solution that was in concert with nature? When did you try to create something with no goal in mind? How did it turn out? When did you create something with a specific goal in mind?

8. Sell Creativity with Charisma

Description: The creative person is a leader, almost by definition. By making something or doing something original, one is showing a new way for others. This is not to be taken lightly. Others may either appreciate or scorn a creative expression, but if it is truly revolutionary, it will most likely not be ignored. Therefore, the creative person's relationship with others associated with the creative endeavor is important. Very few things are done in a vacuum without purpose or influence. This influence is as much determined by the creator as it is by the creation itself. It is helpful if the creative person is in tune with the recipients and is fueled by support to bring a creative expression to fruition.

One attribute of the truly creative individual is their passion. One must enjoy the challenge. Passion is contagious. Others gravitate toward dedication and charisma to reach a goal. The goal should be clear and easily articulated so that it is easy to understand. One can be humble and still be charismatic. Creative people are often labeled eccentric. There is no need to be different for its own sake; do so purposefully where it is warranted.

Book Examples: Throughout the book, both Kim and Dion are creative leaders. They were not only able to exercise creativity, but they were also able to garner support, allowing them to influence the outcome of events. Kim used her leadership skills to help create an atmosphere of success on her baseball team. Similarly, she helped her friends appreciate the value of participation in the school play.

In an analogous way, Dion's creativity on Majestic Mountain helped to influence others to solve problems as they arose. He was able to gain the support of his friends. Their respect for his passion, expressed through his example, helped to make their journey a success.

Points of Discussion: When have you been both a creator and a leader? How was your passion for a creative endeavor spread to others? Have you ever experienced rejection because of creative expression? Do you find it difficult to communicate a creative expression succinctly? That is often a challenge. What creative endeavor could you not have completed without the support of others?

9. Solutions Create New Problems – Creative Evolution

Description: One can never rest on past successes. Invariably, solutions create new problems. An inventor once joked that she creates to fix what she broke from the last creation. Since creativity is the assimilation of somewhat unrelated parts to make something new, it follows an evolutionary path. What was unknown becomes known, so the next assimilation can be based on the newfound knowledge. All art forms follow this evolution to some extent. Often, the more deviant a step is from the natural progression, the harder it is to be understood and accepted by others. Sometimes the collective consciousness needs to 'catch up' over time with the visionary who skipped a couple of steps in the progression of things.

Unpredictable and surprising things can happen in the creative process. Discoveries can be welcomed or scorned. It is important to verify them and then advance with a gentle acceptance of the new reality. It is tempting to refuse to acknowledge the obvious, especially when it is contrary to current beliefs.

Adventuresome behavior often results in unpredictable consequences. One's ability to accept and react appropriately to unpredictability is a necessary component of a creative lifestyle. One must not rest on past successes but rather embrace the new opportunities that it has generated, especially when results are better than expected.

Book Examples: The boys' ability to cross the lake at the flooded bridge over Wandering River led to confusion for Brandon and Phillip. Every action has consequences, and when charting new territory, the consequences are not always readily apparent.

An unanticipated consequence of using paper from the paper drive to get the bonfire started resulted in burning a copy of *The Script* that the Sharefield Gang had worked so hard to recover.

The Sharefield Gang took on the task of cleaning the old mansion, even though they already had several successes to be proud of over that summer. They were not afraid to face a new challenge.

Points of Discussion: When have you created something that had unpredictable consequences? How did you move forward in response to the new situation? When did you engage in a creative expression that was not well understood by others? Did their understanding change over time? Has pride in a past accomplishment ever stalled advancement?

10. Always Remain Optimistic

Description: Creativity takes courage. Often, the hardest part of a creative project is starting to work on it. Creative endeavors require a belief that something of value will result.

There needs to be a certain faith in one's ability to succeed to sustain motivation. Self-defeatists are defeated. Creativity means not having an instruction book. The creator must write the procedures as they go, sometimes feeling like they are drawing a picture with a pencil, and having already shaded the entire page with mistakes, are now faced with erasing that which is not needed to make the image. It is often difficult. Success is never guaranteed. However, the chances of failure, if one stops prematurely or never starts, are one hundred percent. Striving to practice a creative lifestyle is not only hard, but it also takes courage. Further, it is often scrutinized by others who don't immediately understand its significance. The cost versus reward equation is often out of balance, yet the optimist perseveres.

Book Examples: The Sharefield Gang remained optimistic about success. Dion led his friends up Majestic Mountain with the conviction that together, they could resolve any issue that arose. The boys did not want to abandon their mountain journey despite the challenges they faced.

In a similar vein, Chelsea, Kim, and Lucia were able to free Grand Paw through clear thinking and a positive "we can do this" attitude.

Points of Discussion: When have you procrastinated on starting something that you knew would remain undetermined until you finally completed it? Have you found ambiguity to be intimidating? When did a self-defeatist attitude lead to defeat? When were you successful in feeling the fear and moving forward anyway?